THE ANGEL AND THE SWORD

Sigmund Brouwer

HARVEST HOUSE PUBLISHERS

EUGENE, OREGON

Cover by Left Coast Design, Portland, Oregon

Cover image © Cecil G. Rice

THE ANGEL AND THE SWORD
Copyright © 2005 by Sigmund Brouwer
Published by Harvest House Publishers
Eugene, Oregon 97402
www.harvesthousepublishers.com

Library of Congress Cataloging-in-Publication Data

Brouwer, Sigmund, 1959-
    The angel and the sword / Sigmund Brouwer.
      p. cm. — (The guardian angel)
    Summary: In 1351, Raphael, a jester at the papal court in Avignon, France, is falsely accused of trying to kill the reigning Pope Clement VI and, with the help of his guardian angel, must decide whether to trust a beautiful English girl who may or may not be part of the assassination plot.
    ISBN 0-7369-0293-7 (pbk.)
    [1. Guardian angels—Fiction. 2. Fools and jesters—Fiction. 3. Clement VI, Pope, ca. 1291-1352—Fiction. 4. Popes—Fiction. 5. Avignon (Papal city)—Fiction. 6. Angels—Fiction. 7. France—History—John II, 1350-1364—Fiction. 8. Christian life—Fiction.] I. Title. II. Series.
PZ7.B79984Amn 2005
    [Fic]—dc22

2004016661

With Love to Savannah,
you'll always be an angel to me...

Angel Blog

It may not surprise you that angels have names.

What may surprise you is that we have a choice in our names.

And what may surprise you more is that nearly 1100 years ago—as you humans measure time—I respectfully asked our Father for the honor of being named after one of you.

To explain why, I want you to imagine you've been taken hostage. The old-fashioned way. Not the way you see in movies where bank robbers wave a gun around, shouting outside to the police that unless they get the money and a private jet, all the hostages will be severely injured.

(I know about those kinds of movies because now that you humans have reached the twenty-first century, I've been forced to watch DVDs far too often when I'm guarding one of you. Can't you go outside and run around the woods and fields and get into more interesting mischief?)

Since you weren't around a thousand years ago or so, and since I was, take my word for it that the old-fashioned way of hostage-taking was usually very civilized. Although once in a while it would have a gruesome ending…but I'll get to that soon enough.

The way it worked was simple.

For example, a king from one country would send his son to the king of another country and vice versa. Under the care of the other king, each son would be well-treated, as kings generally had plenty of money and whenever they ran short they raised the taxes and took what they needed from the people.

5

Essentially these sons were like loaded guns pointed at the head of each king. (More like loaded bows and arrows, since back then guns still weren't invented, but you know what I mean.) Each king knew that if he did something to severely irritate the other king, the hostage son would be killed. It could get messy. After one king killed the other's son, the second king would retaliate by killing the first king's son. Usually, however, the kings would behave and the ending would be happy all around.

Another example happened with bandits, who were fond of kidnapping rich travelers and then sending letters back home asking for money to release the hostage. This was before cell phones. Before telegraphs. Before trains to deliver letters quickly. In other words, it would often take months for anyone in the rich person's household to discover what had happened. Then months more for their reply to reach the bandits. In the meantime, those bandits needed to keep their hostage alive. Because one thing has not changed among you humans over the centuries: Dead hostages aren't worth much.

You can imagine that often the hostages and bandits would become friends, staying together all those months, especially if the hostages promised extra money for better food and accommodations, which would naturally be shared with the bandits.

So, you say, what would be bad about being taken hostage a few centuries or more ago? There would be no machine guns waved around, no crazed terrorists threatening to send you home in little pieces, no muscle-bound cops more concerned about getting headlines than protecting your wonderful smile. No media helicopters above you filming every second of it and cashing in on your misery.

What's bad?

Not much.

Unless, of course, the people on the other end don't come up with the money to keep your bandits happy. Then comes the gruesome ending I mentioned earlier. Bandits, after all, had reputations to maintain. It would not do them any good at all for the world to discover they would let you go if the money didn't arrive.

Why am I asking you to imagine that you've been taken hostage the old-fashioned way?

Because I'd like you to consider what it would have been like a thousand years ago to be a ten-year-old Spanish boy traveling with your uncle through the lands occupied by the Moors. (Back then, the Moors, who lived south of Spain on the other side of the Mediterranean Sea, were considered the bad guys by the rest of Europe, mainly because the Moors were good at winning wars whenever Europe tried to take land from them.) I can't even tell you why the uncle was traveling through the dangerous land, but after they were captured, I think it's easy to guess why he had his ten-year-old nephew with him. This uncle made a deal with the bandits to leave behind the ten-year-old as a hostage for ransom money that the uncle would send as soon as he got back to Spain.

There you are. Ten years old. You wave goodbye to your uncle because he promises to send back money and save you from the bandits. Every night you pray to our Father for protection, and, as time goes by, you discover the bandits are not going to hurt you. Still you pray because you have a deep faith in our Father, and you recognize that when He sent His Son, Jesus, it was the greatest gift in the history of the world.

A year passes. Your uncle is now safe in Spain, hundreds of miles away from the bandits with their big, curved swords—but no money has arrived. You blame it on slow transportation. Old, weak horses maybe.

Two years pass. Still no money. You hope it's because your uncle lost the address and is trying to fix the problem.

By the third year you are beginning to think maybe your uncle has decided he'd rather keep the money than get you back. Unfortunately the Moor bandits come to the same conclusion and they don't want to wait any longer. Fortunately after all this time together, they have formed a great deal of affection for you.

So they offer you your freedom. And a reward.

This you like.

But then the bandits say something that makes you sad and afraid. To get this freedom and reward, you must denounce your Christian faith. You must publicly say that you don't believe that our Father sent His Son, Jesus. You must publicly say that you don't believe Jesus and His death and resurrection is the way to reach our Father both in this life and on the other side of this life.

Worse, if you don't denounce your Christian faith and choose their faith, they will apply a sharp and fast-moving sword to the back of your neck. And that's if you are lucky. Torture is far worse.

What do you do? Take the money and the freedom? (And life!)

Or do you choose to boldly declare your faith in our Father and His Son, who has listened to your prayers every night for the three years of your captivity? Do you choose this, knowing that it will cost you your life, even though you are only 13?

We angels, who constantly cross the border into your physical world, fully understand that giving up your human life to enter into the presence of our Father is far less of a sacrifice than you can comprehend.

On the other hand, because we travel across the border so often, we do understand that most of you lack the perspective to understand this. Because all you know is life as you see it around you, you are unaware of how great it is in the glory of our Father.

So we sympathize with you humans when you face the choice between faith and death, even as we pray that you hold onto your faith.

I can tell you that I mourned for the boy among the bandits who faced his own difficult choice.

You see, I had been sent to guard him since birth, and especially during the three years of captivity. I was there when he lifted his eyes to look into the faces of those who threatened to kill him for his faith. I was there when the tears streamed down his cheeks as he said he could not denounce our Father and His Son, Jesus. I was there when he bravely walked into the prison to face the days of torture waiting him. I was there as he screamed in agony. I was there as our Father's love gave him peace beyond words in the last hours of his earthly life.

I was there because I was waiting to discover if our Father's purpose for me in that moment was to rescue the boy from that torture. And as I waited and grieved over the pain inflicted on his young body, I understood the real reason I'd been sent was to preserve the boy over the three years so that he would have this chance to show the strength of his faith.

I cannot give you what you humans want as a happy ending. The boy died. He became a martyr.

On our side, however, he was immediately greeted with great joy. And of all who witnessed his bravery and faith on earth, a dozen more were so impressed that they too became believers to join us in our

Father's presence at the end of their lives. The Evil One, whom you call Satan, had hoped to defeat the boy; instead, the boy's faith defeated Satan and snatched all those other souls from his horrible grip.

I tell you all of this for two reasons.

Reason one: My request was granted when I asked to be honored with the name of this boy. Pelagius. Among the angels, this is what I am called, and all understand the reason for it.

Reason two: When I am sent to guard one of you, I do not know the ending until it arrives.

It was no different four centuries later in Avignon, France—A.D. 1351 to be exact—where I'd been sent to watch over another boy named Raphael, who lived a lonely life, although he would never admit this to himself.

Because I'd been with Raphael since his early childhood and could read the thoughts on his face as clearly as if he spoke them to me, I am able to relate to you the events that were about to change his life...

1

A gentle cooing from the balcony reminded Raphael that he had lain awake in bed too long as he imagined the faraway streets of Paris. Pigeons, then, first brought him to the window that morning—not the knowledge of the man armed with a deadly crossbow on a nearby rooftop.

"My friends," he called out to the pigeons, "I'll be but a moment."

Raphael threw back his blankets, swung his legs from the bed, winced at the sharpness of cold stone against his bare feet, and rose and stretched, hands high. Sunlight from the window cast his shadow against the wall. As Raphael began to yawn, he wiggled his fingers to make the silhouette of his hands become the shape of a dog's head. Halfway through his yawn, Raphael snapped his mouth shut and dropped his hands.

He looked around his small room in puzzlement.

The cooing outside persisted.

"Patience, my friends," he said with good humor. "I face a mystery."

A mystery indeed. Where were his clothes? Not the colorful tights and vest that he wore as a jester when entertaining the court—those were plainly in sight on the wall hook. It was the regular tunic and pants that Raphael wanted—today was Easter Sunday and he needed to dress for a stroll through the town.

Where *were* his clothes?

Not on the chair where he'd set them the previous evening before blowing out the candle and falling asleep. Not on the floor. And not—Raphael pulled the curled blankets apart—lost among the bed covers.

The room was barely large enough for his straw bed, the chair now empty of clothes, and a small table which held a chunk of hard bread, a pitcher of water, and a chamber pot. If Raphael couldn't see the pants and tunic, he could rightly conclude neither were in the room.

Very strange.

He grinned to himself. Obviously someone had played a jest on the jester. One of the ladies-in-waiting perhaps. Or Claude, the cook's assistant.

Yes, Raphael told himself, Jean-Claude had taken the clothes. Hadn't it been yesterday that Raphael asked Jean-Claude if his ears were dirty? All the others in the kitchen had laughed when Raphael pulled an egg from Jean-Claude's ear. It was an easy trick, really, palming the egg from a nearby basket and with a flick of the wrist pretending it had suddenly appeared from the side of Jean-Claude's head. Not a mean trick either, yet Jean-Claude had sulked, walked away, and refused Raphael's apologies.

No clothes.

Raphael shrugged and reached for his jester's costume. It would hardly do to prance down the hallway undressed as he searched for the other clothing. Too many other members of the courts and their servants occupied this wing of the Palace of the Popes. That would be exactly what Claude hoped to have happen.

Besides, Raphael's friends stood outside on the edge of the balcony. He rarely kept them waiting. He also knew that it had taken months to train the pigeons to appear at this time of day. It would not do any good to disappoint them, not even once, for who knew if they would return then the next morning.

"Yes, my friends," he said as he hopped about on one leg, pulling his tights onto the other. "I have bread for you."

Tights overtop of socks, one green, the other yellow. Then shirt with stripes to match his tights. Vest overtop, cinched with a band at the waist. And because it was habit, he placed on his head the jester's cap with the cloth balls that jiggled when Raphael juggled.

Raphael was big—unusual for a jester because most depended on the quickness and agility possessed by the small. It only made it more entertaining and unexpected when someone his size juggled or did backflips or balanced on a rope. He had thick blond hair that always fell into matted curls, and a wide-open face that always seemed to be smiling. The smile seemed to attract many of the maids and kitchen servants, although he was rarely aware of it.

Dressed now and wearing his usual smile, Raphael snatched the chunk of hard bread from the table and moved to his balcony windows to lean outside.

"Good morning, little ones," he said.

The pigeons hopped toward him. Raphael looked them over. Three today. The fat white one who never failed to appear. A gray one, head cocked sideways. And…why the third one was very small.

Raphael clucked at the fat white pigeon. "Mother Josephine, is this one a child of yours?"

Mother Josephine did not answer. Mother Josephine was intent on the tiny pieces of bread that Raphael slowly tore loose and set on the edge of the balcony.

With strutting steps and bobbing head, Mother Josephine reached the bread ahead of the other two pigeons and stabbed her beak downward.

Raphael laughed softly. He tore more tiny pieces loose and set them behind Mother Josephine. The pigeon was long accustomed to him and did not take flight as his hand moved above her. The other two pigeons pecked at his offerings.

"It is good to see you again, my friends," he said as he continued to feed them. "Good to see you indeed."

As Raphael spoke in low, reassuring tones, he let his eyes sweep across the view from his balcony. Even with his eyes closed, he could have described the sights, for he had lived in the room since boyhood.

There was Mount Ventoux to the northwest, its rounded top like a huge mound at the horizon visible between palace towers. There were the rooftops below, red clay tile weathered to almost gray. Balconies and ledges among the maze of buildings. All comfortable and familiar landmarks.

Yet this morning, when Raphael swept his eyes over Avignon, he saw none of what he usually took in. For this morning, squarely in his line of sight, there was a man on the clay tiles of a nearby roof.

This man was lying almost at the edge of the roof. He peered downward into the courtyard. From Raphael's viewpoint, it was impossible to see what the man was studying down in the courtyard with such care.

That mattered little to Raphael.

This man was dressed as a soldier. Full armor. Long broadsword. Helmet nearby.

What frightened Raphael most was the remaining piece of military equipment beside this soldier. The crossbow. Capable of slamming an arrow through a knight's armor. Capable of sending an arrow right through a deer.

Even as Raphael watched, this soldier loaded the bow, bracing it to pull the arrow into place, and set the crossbow beside him. Then the man looked downward into the courtyard again. Whatever he was hunting from there, it was not a deer.

This was no soldier.

But an assassin.

2

Raphael drew breath to shout warning.

Warning?

How could any words help someone unseen in the court-yard that far away? Or what if the assassin was waiting for his prey to appear? How then would his words warn someone not yet in the courtyard? With those thoughts, Raphael decided any warning now would simply alert the assassin.

Raphael reacted without thinking further.

He waved away the pigeons. At first they fixed their black eyes on his hands and searched for more bread crumbs. Raphael was forced to push them off the ledge before they took flight.

Raphael winced and hoped that the assassin had not heard the sudden sound of their wings clapping against air.

The assassin did not move from his position.

Raphael ducked back into his room and grabbed two juggling pins. These he could use as weapons to stun the assassin. Raphael darted back to his window and clambered out onto the balcony railing.

Child's play, he told himself, to reach the soldier. After all, was he not a court jester, trained in acrobats? He need merely climb across this balcony onto the one beside. Then drop to one below. From there, it was a simple matter of running along a ledge to the end of this wing of the palace and then crossing a stone beam to the roof of the building that held the assassin. While a single misstep meant plunging to his death three stories below, the possibility of falling meant little, not to one with the skills of a jester.

Child's play? Only if the assassin did not hear Raphael's approach. Only if the deadly crossbow was not turned in his direction as Raphael balanced himself—open and exposed as the ideal target—across the stone beam.

Raphael forced those thoughts out of his mind. He had to act quickly, for no assassin would risk imprisonment or hanging to shoot someone as common as a servant. And here in the courtyards of the Palace of the Popes there were many men of considerable political importance. Who was it at risk? Who was about to be murdered?

Questions later, Raphael told himself.

He tucked the juggling pins into the back of his tights. Hands free, he was able to climb quickly from one balcony to the next. Moments later he dropped to the balcony lower down.

A startled gasp drew his attention.

Raphael turned his head to glance through the open window into the room. He locked eyes with someone his height, someone he had never seen before at the Palace. She stood at the side of her bed in a long gown, brushing her long hair, her right hand frozen in midstroke.

In that moment, it seemed Raphael could not find the strength to draw breath into his lungs. Beautiful? She was beyond beautiful to him. The long hair that she held in her left hand, ready to brush, was raven black. Her eyes were deep blue, more perfect than any sapphire. Her lips, the blooming of a rose. Raphael knew he could recite poetry about the wonder of the features of her face, but more than that was the way she watched him with poise, a grace that suggested mystery.

In that moment, Raphael nearly forgot about an assassin on a nearby rooftop. And in that moment, she stepped forward and angrily closed the window in his face.

It startled him so much that he nearly fell backward off the balcony. Only instinct and years of training saved him, a quick shifting of weight that was almost a hop in midair. He landed softly and pushed off without pause, using his momentum to drop from the balcony onto the ledge that ran down the length of this wing of the palace.

Raphael was thankful for the supple and expensive leather of his perfectly fitted shoes. His feet did not so much as scuff the slightest sound when he landed—this was not the moment to give the assassin warning.

Raphael crouched and ran the length of the ledge almost as fast as a man might run along the ground below. The balance required Raphael's total concentration. The beautiful stranger's face left his mind, as did everything except for the demands of his silent, crouching run across a beam no wider than a dinner plate.

He reached the end of the ledge and dropped to the stone beam that led across to the next building.

Now only a perilous crossing separated him from the assassin.

Raphael measured the distance. Too far to throw a juggling pin. He would be forced to cross, unable to defend himself if the assassin heard him, unable to dodge a deadly crossbow arrow.

As Raphael looked across, he discovered he could now see what the assassin viewed in the courtyard below. He could see the assassin's target.

The pope.

Pope Clement VI. Perhaps the most important man in all of Europe.

The assassin had yet to lift his crossbow. Because of someone who stood in front of the pope?

Raphael did not pause to question further the assassin's delay. The pope's remaining life might now be measured in heartbeats.

Raphael reached for the juggling pins, pulled them from his waistband so that he carried one in each hand, and began to sprint across the beam.

The slap of his running feet was too loud! Surely the assassin would take warning!

Raphael knew too well the possibility but could not stop. He must risk it. The pope was in danger.

A second later, the assassin began to turn his head. A tiny squeak of leather on smooth stone must have caught his ear.

Still too far away to attack, Raphael took the only desperate action he could. Without breaking stride, he threw the juggling pin from his left hand in an underhanded motion.

Given warning, the assassin ducked. The pin bounced off the roof just above his head and fell downward into the courtyard.

The assassin completed his turn with unbelievable quickness, and in one motion he scooped the crossbow into position.

"Stop," he hissed at Raphael.

Raphael told himself to dive into the crossbow. He told himself the heroic action would at least save the pope's life, that when his body tumbled into the courtyard, it would raise alarm.

Yet the crossbow arrow was pointed directly at his heart, and much as he tried to force himself to continue, Raphael found himself pulling up short.

"You would be the hero, Raphael?" the assassin jeered softly.

Raphael could not reply. He stared at the unwavering crossbow and heaved for breath. This high up, both the heaving and the assassin's words could not be heard below. The pope remained in danger.

A shout proved him wrong.

"Who goes up there?"

Raphael had forgotten about his juggling pin. It must have landed in the courtyard somewhere near the pope!

"The…alarm…has…sounded," Raphael managed to gasp.

Another cry from below.

"So it appears." The assassin smiled. His hair, dark and curling behind the ears, framed a narrow face and glittering eyes. Hooked nose. A cold smile of large white teeth contrasted with the deeply tanned skin of his face. The smile sent a shiver through Raphael.

The assassin's smile grew wider.

Raphael saw the man's knuckle whiten on the trigger of the crossbow. *The whitening of pressure!*

Time stopped for Raphael. He fully expected the click of a released arrow, the hiss of air, and then a crunch of bone as it hit his chest.

The assassin shot.

But he'd spun the crossbow without warning and sent the arrow harmlessly into the center of the courtyard.

Raphael unfroze and managed to breathe again.

The assassin set the bow down on the roof.

"Here it is, jester. Take it."

With that, the assassin sprung to his feet and took three sprinting steps to the open window that had let him first gain entry to the roof.

Soldiers' voices began to fill the courtyard, but they were hidden from sight by the roof.

"Goodbye, jester," the assassin taunted as he closed the window.

Those words broke Raphael loose from his stunned spell. He darted the last few steps across the beam to the roof, grabbed the crossbow, turned back and fought the slope of the roof until he reached the window.

Locked.

"Who goes there?" came a deep voice from the courtyard. "Shout out now!"

Raphael pounded disappointment onto the roof with his fist.

"Who goes there?" The voice was louder. Angrier.

Raphael sighed. He crawled back to the edge of the roof.

"It is I," Raphael called down as he peered again into the courtyard. A half dozen soldiers waited in a spread-out circle, all peering upward at the roof. Some were armed with broadswords. Others with crossbows. Those with crossbows had their weapons aimed upward.

Raphael ducked back from instinct.

An arrow whizzed past the edge of the roof.

"Shoot no more!" Raphael cried. "I mean no harm!"

"Then throw down your weapon!" the deep voice commanded.

Without thinking, Raphael did just that. Moments later, he heard it clatter among the soldiers.

Minutes later, the window to the roof opened, and the same deep voice commanded him to step inside.

Raphael did, glad to be off the roof. Once standing inside, he blinked, trying to find vision in the shadows of the room after the brightness of the sun outside.

As his feet touched the floor, the soldier with the deep voice pinned the end of his sword to Raphael's throat.

"You would kill the pope, jester?"

Raphael began to protest.

The sword pressed into his skin, bringing the pain of pierced skin.

"Not another word," the soldier said, "or you will taste this steel."

He turned his head and spoke to other soldiers that Raphael was just now able to distinguish among the shadows.

"Bind him," the soldier ordered the others, "as the criminal scum that he is."

Angel Blog

As an angel, I wanted to suddenly appear and protest the injustice of the accusation against Raphael. He had been put solely in my charge and would continue to be my responsibility until I was commanded otherwise by our Father.

That would have been fun and satisfying.

Satisfying because my first reaction was this anger. I loved Raphael as much as you would love your own children—I had been watching over him from the days when he'd been crying for his mother's milk.

And fun because I'm sure the soldiers—so proud of their strength and authority and military weapons—would have scattered in all directions like mice in front of a barking dog.

After all, there's nothing like the unexpected appearance of a bright, shimmering light in the form of a supernatural being to remind you humans of what you already subconsciously know and fear: There is a spiritual world that you cannot see and can only vaguely sense in moments when you stop focusing on your selfish wants.

But as the soldiers surrounded Raphael, our Father did not direct me to intervene in any manner.

Not for a moment did I consider our Father's plan to be wrong in any fashion, nor did I question His decision to have me remain as an invisible observer. Our Father's infinite wisdom is always proved right by the passage of time.

Besides, even if I had wanted to help Raphael, I would have been far more limited than you might expect.

This is as good a time as any to explain something about angels. It's my standard lecture about angels, and I'm too efficient (some of you might call it lazy, but I'll stick with efficient) to try to word it differently from one time to another, so skip through if you already know it. And certainly don't stop me if you've heard it already.

Angels can't create. That's something only our Father can do. As I'll say whenever possible, if you could have been there at the beginning, you would be the biggest believer in the universe. Yes, *that* beginning. Of time. Of the universe. Not that I was there. But the great thing about the spiritual world is that time and space don't form a prison for us like they do for you. (Believe me, you'll find out someday. On the other side. By then you'll be glad you trusted in our Father.)

As I was saying, since time and space don't bind us, we angels have a good idea of what it was like at the beginning of creation. "Spectacular" doesn't give it justice. It's beyond comprehension. Then again, if you television watchers got off the couch and walked through the woods and took a close look at our Father's handiwork, you might get an inkling of how incredible it was.

What else can't angels do?

Angels can't change substances. Again, only our Father can do that. So don't come to me and ask for that lump of lead to be changed into gold. I'm not a fairy godmother. And yes, I've had that request before.

Angels can't alter the laws of nature. Only our Father can.

Same thing for miracles.

And here's something that might surprise you. Angels can't see into your hearts. (After centuries and centuries of experience with you humans, however, we can make some pretty good guesses.) Some of you wise guys might be saying, hey, no problem, any good doctor can get a good view of the human heart. But that's not the heart I'm talking about—and you know it.

Angels can't change your hearts either. Remember that thing called "choice"?

Anyway, that's a lot of what we can't do.

Keep that in mind, because the fallen angels can't do any of it either. Fallen angels. That would be Satan and his gang. They can't do any of our Father's special stuff either. No creating out of nothing, no changing of substances, no altering the laws of nature. No searching or changing the hearts of men.

Why's that important to remember?

Too many humans worry about demons because they believe demons have special power. Not so. Good thing, because I have plenty of stories about their bad intentions and how we'd been sent in by our Father to protect you against them. Nasty bunch, those guys. Of course, they've known for a long time that when they picked sides, they joined a loser—Satan himself. For eternity. That would make anyone bitter.

Here's what's really important to remember about the fallen angels: Misery loves company.

They want as many of you to lose your souls to the Evil One as possible. They cackle with hideous glee every time one of you dies before making a faith decision in our Father. It's hard to decide what they like most—the horror that overwhelms you on the other side when you immediately comprehend what it will be like to spend eternity among them or the shock when you discover there was more to life on earth than life on earth.

For the most part, then, an angel's job is to protect you long enough for you to make your decision. Do you want eternal light? Or eternal darkness? Yes, your earthly life has great value to our

Father—that's why He designed it for you to be able to enjoy so many things about it. But far more important to Him is the destination of your soul. What you do with your choices. And don't fool yourself. All of you choose. Deciding not to choose is just like choosing against Him.

Raphael still had not shown anything in his life to indicate faith in our Father. Because of that, with the soldiers around him, I suspected I would be called to protect Raphael if they actually threatened his life.

Otherwise, I could expect to do what I'd already been doing for years around him.

Wait and watch.

Watch and wait...

3

Raphael stood, alone and hands bound, in the pope's study chamber. In any other circumstances, he would have been overjoyed at the privilege. Few were those granted public audience with the pope, let alone invited into his private study.

The ceiling was arched stone, and the floors were of exquisite tile. On the walls, a huge mural of forest life showed falcon, ferret, and stag hunting, bird snaring, and even fishing in a fish tank. How wonderful! Raphael could entertain the kitchen girls for hours with the description of all that he was seeing here in—

He cut his silent admiration short. To entertain he first must be allowed to rejoin his friends, and the rough rope that held his wrists together was a painful reminder that he might never see them again. A painful reminder of the soldiers' rough treatment as they'd shoved him down the hallways earlier to reach the chamber.

The injustice!

Raphael vowed he would find a way to prove his innocence.

The scraping of the door to the chamber interrupted his thoughts. Raphael waited for the guards who usually escorted Pope Clement VI.

None stepped inside.

Instead it was the pope himself who shuffled to his desk and sat behind it to look at Raphael with some interest.

Raphael's heart sank. He had not been invited to kiss the pope's ring, an action of honor and respect.

"You are…?" Clement VI asked.

"One of the court jesters, m'lord."

Pope Clement VI sighed. Without his papal dress and papal staff, he seemed smaller than Raphael had imagined. Of course this was the first time he had really met Clement VI.

Raphael discovered too that the pope was balding. His head was a dome, gray hair on the sides. His nose was almost like that of an eagle, but wider. And the eyes, lost in wrinkles of tiredness, were as fierce as an eagle's.

Now those eyes bored into Raphael. "Here in Avignon," Clement VI said, "hundreds of maids and servants attend to the needs of the papal court, dozens of musicians and jesters. You will forgive me if I do not know your name."

"Raphael, m'lord."

The pope's eyes widened slightly. "I have heard of a jester named Raphael who stood atop the highest tower of the palace and juggled no less than five balls. Would you be *that* Raphael?"

"Yes, m'lord."

"And your family name?"

"Villenuve, m'lord. Raphael de Villenuve. And I am innocent of the charges. Rather it was—"

"Silence," the pope commanded. "This is a private meeting. I do not wear the robes of my office. Despite the informality, you will not speak unless it is to answer my questions."

Raphael bowed his head.

"De Villenuve…" Clement VI spoke as if he were thinking aloud. "Do we not have a Villenuve in Rome? A courtier?"

"My father, your worship," Raphael answered as he lifted his head again.

Clement VI glared at him. Briefly. Then softened. "I did ask a question, didn't I."

Raphael nodded.

"I'm told you tried to kill me. Is that true?"

"No, m'lord!"

"I understand why you would speak so firmly," Clement VI replied. "Not only do you face the penalty of death but so does your family."

Until this moment Raphael had not even considered that reality. A political assassination was so vile—and so often tried—that to prevent it, punishment was often extended to include the criminal's immediate family.

"Tell me, Raphael," Clement VI was saying, "why do you deny the attempt? You shot an arrow into the courtyard—I saw it myself. You were found with the weapon."

"I did not fire the crossbow, m'lord."

Raphael then explained what had happened.

Clement VI regarded him thoughtfully. "You claim you *threw* the juggling pin. Yet the captain of the guards tells me that the dropped juggling pin was a ploy to get me to step back from the woman who had my attention and look upward, making it easier for you to find the target."

Raphael watched Clement VI but bit his tongue against the urge to speak.

"Well," Clement VI said, "have you no answer to that?"

"I was waiting for a question, m'lord."

Clement VI smiled and then let Raphael finish.

"And my answer, m'lord, is that it may appear to have happened how your captain described. But told my way, there is also truth."

"Truth without proof. No one but you saw the assassin. Is that not so?"

Raphael thought a thunderclap had struck him, the answer came so clearly.

"I do have a witness!"

"Who?"

Raphael told Clement VI of the girl who had slammed a window in his face—but he did not mention that her beauty had struck him equally hard as he stood on her balcony. "She, m'lord, can confirm my story."

Clement VI raised a bell from his desk and tinkled it once. Within seconds, a guard opened the door. Clement VI instructed the guard to bring them the girl as described by Raphael. The guard departed.

They were left in long minutes of silence that Raphael dared not break. He shifted his weight from foot to foot, unable to contain his nervousness.

Clement VI occupied himself with papers on his desk. He took a quill, dipped it into ink, and signed three of the sheaves of paper.

"You may find it strange," Clement VI said without lifting his head, "that you and I speak so informally. After all, my office demands of me much ceremony."

Raphael did not hear a question in the pope's words, so he waited.

"I regret the need to keep this matter away from public audience," Clement VI continued, "because it means I must be sole judge of the entire matter. And, as it was my life in danger, I am not without bias. However..."

Clement VI again directed his gaze at Raphael. "There are some papal matters of great importance that are in delicate negotiations. It will do no good for word of an attempt on my life to reach certain ears. And, as no one but a small group of guards witnessed the attempt, it is a secret that will be kept."

Raphael fought the chills that rippled beneath his skin. Something in the pope's tone was a warning. He did not have long to wait.

"You see, I have no choice. Even if I believe you are innocent of the attempt, I must imprison you—secretly—until the negotiations are complete. That is my only guarantee you will speak of it to no one else."

Clement VI rubbed his face as if weary of his responsibilities. "And if I believe you are guilty, you will be executed in equal secrecy."

Raphael forgot himself and spoke without waiting for a question. "M'lord, I—"

"Silence." Clement VI resumed his examination of the papers on his desk.

It seemed to Raphael that an hour passed before a respectful knock on the door disturbed the quiet of the room.

"Enter," Clement VI said.

It was not, as Raphael had expected, the guard who had first entered, but the captain of the guard, who had first put a sword to his throat.

He was large and filled the entire doorway. In his right hand, he carried a large cloth sack. A frown covered his massive face and made his looks appear even darker. When he opened his mouth to speak, Raphael saw that several teeth were missing, broken off as if once struck by the blows of a war club.

"She is with me, your worship," the captain said.

"Bring her in."

"And I have other news." He hefted the sack to indicate the news.

"Pertaining to the jester?" Clement VI asked.

"Yes, your worship."

"Join us and close the door behind you then."

Raphael did not think to wonder what the other news might be or what was in the sack. After all, he was innocent and he knew it. Besides, the one with raven hair was a great distraction.

She curtsied to Clement VI.

His face softened at her young loveliness.

"Your name?" he asked gently.

"Juliana of Normandy, your worship." Her French was faultless, but she spoke with an accent. Raphael, who had never been outside of Avignon, could not decide where the accent might have come from.

"Ah, yes, the delegates from England," Clement VI said, answering Raphael's silent question. "I trust your lodgings are satisfactory?"

"Most satisfactory, your worship."

"You were not disturbed earlier this morning?" he asked her.

Raphael tensed. Now, at last, he would be cleared.

Puzzlement filled her features. She had not yet bothered to glance over at Raphael.

"Disturbed, your worship? Here in the Palace of the Popes?"

Clement VI glanced sharply at Raphael. Then back to Juliana.

"Look upon this young man," he told her. "Is his face not familiar?"

She stared. Raphael stared at her. Inside he pleaded for her to speak out for him.

"Perhaps, your worship. But there are so many strangers to me here that I…"

"He claims he stood on your balcony earlier this morning."

Juliana merely continued to stare at Raphael.

"And on the roof behind me," Raphael cried, "did you not see a man armed with a crossbow!"

The captain stepped forward and slapped Raphael across the face, a blow hard enough to break the skin at the sides of his mouth. "Silence!"

Raphael licked his blood away, and still she stared at him.

"Juliana?" Clement VI prompted.

"Now that I look closely, m'lord," she began slowly.

"Yes?"

Raphael's heart raced. Not only did his own life depend on her next words but his family's future did too.

She nodded to herself, as if confirming her thoughts, and she spoke with great seriousness. "Now that I look closely," she finished, "I have never seen him before."

4

"M'lady—"

Another backhanded blow from the burly captain slammed Raphael's protest short.

No expression crossed Juliana's face as she watched blood trickle from his split lip.

"You have my gratitude for assisting us with this matter," Clement VI said to her, "and my apologies that we interrupted your morning."

Juliana of Normandy curtsied again, and, at the captain's invitation, departed through the study door.

"A desperate attempt, jester," the captain sneered as he closed the door and turned back to Raphael and Clement VI, "hoping that out of pity, she might lie for you."

Raphael stared back. He could feel the blood now on his chin, but he was too angry to show any weakness by attempting to wipe it away.

The captain lifted the sack that he'd set down near the door. "Your worship," he went on, "I believe this will demonstrate further the lies of this villainous jester."

Clement VI raised a questioning eyebrow. "Yes, Alfred?"

In response, the captain dumped the contents of the sack onto the tiled floor.

Raphael drew in a quick breath.

"Your clothes, I believe," Alfred said.

"Yes!" Raphael could not hide his surprise. "How did—"

"You would be a fool to deny them as such," Alfred said, "for we have a sound witness that testifies they are yours."

"They were missing from my room when I woke this morning!"

"Of course," the captain grunted in mock agreement. "And your provisions were missing too?"

"Provisions? I do not understand."

"Playing the fool will not help, jester." The captain turned to Clement VI. "Your eminence, we found the clothing and provisions in a saddlebag on a horse at the stables."

"I was not there!" cried Raphael, his anger forgotten in his confusion.

Alfred faced Raphael. "Why then does the stablemaster say you met with him last night? Why then does he say you purchased from him his fastest horse and requested that he have it waiting for you?"

"No! Those are falsehoods!"

The captain turned back to Clement VI. "Were I him, m'lord, I would have committed the crime costumed as the jester. Then in fleeing I would clothe myself in less color, for the soldiers would be searching the town for one in jester's garb."

Clement VI nodded. "There is logic in that. A horse waiting, and a disguise too."

"No!" Raphael protested.

Clement VI and Alfred ignored him and continued their conversation.

"Not only his fastest horse and provisions for two days, your worship, but this…" The guard reached into the sack and pulled from it a small leather bag, bulging with weight. "We found this in his room." He emptied it onto Clement VI's desk.

Raphael gasped at the glitter of tumbling silver coin.

"Payment, I suspect," the captain said. "Like Judas of old, he was happy to betray you to your death for mere silver."

"No!" Raphael cried again. He could think of nothing else to say.

Clement VI looked away from the silver and into Raphael's eyes.

"Who bought you?" he asked Raphael. "Who gave you this payment to take my life?"

"M'lord! It is not my silver. I am innocent."

Alfred coughed.

"Yes?" Clement VI said.

"There was also this in his room—a letter." Alfred held up a sheet of paper. "With instructions to kill you by a certain date."

"I've never read the letter!" Raphael said. "Never seen it!"

"It appears," Alfred said, ignoring Raphael's outburst, "to have come from a leading Italian banker."

"The Italians!" Clement VI was angry. He turned to Raphael. "You are Italian. Help us find your master, and I will spare your family."

His mother, Raphael thought. His two sisters. His father. Each would be taken without mercy from their home. Each killed horribly. And worse, each would blame it on him as they died.

"No…" Raphael moaned his agony.

"No? You will not tell?" Clement VI tightened his mouth with fury and was barely able to speak from clenched teeth. "Perhaps the whip will loosen your tongue."

Clement VI barked an order to the captain. "I have seen and heard enough. Take him below. To the dungeon."

———

Below. To the dungeon.

Raphael sat in chains, aware that he was prisoner beneath a tower so imposing that it dominated the courtyard and the rest of the palace and all of Avignon, a tower so staggeringly high that someone at the top could drop a rock, and count slowly almost to three until that rock hit the ground far below.

It was known far and wide as the Tower of Angels, one of the most secure fortifications in all of Europe. The top chambers of this tower, where Clement VI had so recently judged Raphael, contained the pope's study and living quarters.

If this weren't reason enough for the tower to be filled with men-at-arms, directly below the pope's study and living quarters was the chamberlain's chamber, and *he*, after the pope, was the second most powerful person in all Christendom.

And if this weren't yet reason enough, on ground level— below the chamberlain's chamber and above the dungeon—was the Treasury Hall, where all of the kingdom's taxes were counted and stored.

Reason enough for security—the pope's quarters, the chamberlain's quarters, the treasury hall, and the dungeon—that this tower's walls were as thick as not one stride, not two strides, but fully as thick as three walking strides of a large man.

Perhaps after years of siege Avignon itself could fall, and much later even the palace within Avignon, but no army would ever topple this Tower of Angels.

Raphael found little comfort in knowing that his new living quarters were so secure. He found even less in thinking of Clement VI so far above him, comfortable in his elegant quarters—and alive!—while Raphael, who had saved his life, endured the cold clammy darkness of the dungeon.

Hours passed.

Raphael had no sense of time, not without the sun or shadows to guide him. Putrid water dripped onto his head. He breathed shallowly through his mouth, trying to avoid the stench of accumulated body wastes. Moaning of distant prisoners added to his horror. But nothing in the dungeon filled him with as much fear as did the thoughts of the fate that would fall on his family.

In two weeks, three weeks, as little time as it took for messengers to reach Italy, his mother would be taken at sword point from her garden. His mother, who had kissed all his hurts during his boyhood, who had sobbed for days before his departure to Avignon. She would be helpless to fight her death.

His sisters too. Raphael nearly cried in the darkness to remember the songs they always sang for him. Rosy-cheeked Marie. Dark-haired Elizabeth. Soon they would be old enough to be married—it had been that long since he'd departed—but instead of the joy of betrothal, each would now hang.

And his father. So strong and noble. With that special smile of pride for him during the quiet times they had shared. He had encouraged him to be the best, to accept his training in Avignon as the beginning of a wonderful life. Instead of continued warm pride, his father would receive death by rope.

Each would believe that Raphael had betrayed God, his country, and them.

Which would be worse to them, Raphael tortured himself with his thoughts, *death itself, or hearing of the betrayal?*

In the darkness, a rat ran across his leg. Then another.

Raphael had heard of rats attacking unguarded babies in cribs. Was he any less helpess, his arms and legs chained against stone wall? If he fell asleep, would they attack him?

Raphael fought the chains and cried out against the injustice. After all, he had tried to save Clement VI, not murder him. Why was this happening?

No one answered his cries.

The chains did not loosen.

And time passed as slowly as the steady drip of water on his head.

He could find no hope.

Raphael with no hope?

Let me break in for a moment (not that you have a choice).

Over the centuries, I've spent a lot of time with many of you. All of you I've loved, but some of you have been difficult to like.

You might ask how can you love someone but not like him.

Easy.

Love flows from our Father. It is an eternally unbreakable bond and the strongest force in the universe. We angels, like our Father, are able to love you and your souls in a way that you'll never understand until you cross the border to our side.

But there are days when you are extremely difficult to like. Let me count the ways that you are able to irritate an angel watching over you. (We're not bothered by things like the moments that you pick your nose. Or when you scratch your armpit and then sniff your finger. Those are parts of the physical world, and, hey, you're built in a way that makes that sort of stuff inevitable.)

The things that irritate us come from your selfishness. Your whining. Complaining. Bullying. Lying. Mean-spiritedness. If you see a pattern here, good for you. If you don't, I'll spell it out.

All of the things I've just mentioned are choices that defy love. No coincidence that Jesus told you the two greatest commands were to love our Father with all your heart, soul, and mind, and to love your fellow man as you would love yourself.

Love. Love. Love.

Choices based on love, like generosity, kindness, and justice, are all very pleasing to our Father. Choices that hurt you or others because those choices don't reflect His love are, well, hurtful to Him, and at the very least irritating to us angels.

But out of all the sins that irritate me, there's one near the top of my list. One that might surprise you, and the fact that it is surprising irritates me even more.

Worry.

You don't hear worry called a sin too often, do you?

You get the standard sins listed all the time. Don't steal. Don't lust. Yada, yada, yada.

But how often do your elders tell you that worrying is a sin?

Not enough.

Hey, when you worry, when you believe there is no hope, it is a very strong way of silently telling our Father that you don't trust Him and His plans.

Believe me, that's an insult to Him, who is all powerful and is weaving all the human events together in a way that works to His greater glory. In other words, when you get to this side, you'll see how ridiculous your worries were.

Face it, no matter how much you worry, it's not going to change one simple fact: You're going to die. Whether sooner or later, whether quickly or slowly, you're going to check out of this world. Buy the ranch. Kick the bucket.

Not only that, death is going to take away whatever wealth and possessions you might have. You're going to leave behind all the people you love. It's going to wipe you from the face of this earth.

Depressing, huh.

Just ask Job. You know, the guy in the Bible. Lost his sheep, horses, cows, children, and on top of all that got some horrible itchy diseases. What Job learned, however, is a great lesson. Our Father and His love is what matters most. That's what's waiting for you when you lose everything. And you *will* lose everything, if I haven't made that clear enough yet.

So why worry? One, everything is in our Father's hands and will work out to the good of those who have faith in Him. Two, your ultimate hope is in what He promises through His Son. Whether you live ten years or a hundred, whether you live in a mansion or a hut, when you get to our side, you're going to discover a whole new existence that's going to make whatever bad things happened on earth seem like a distant memory.

I trust you're getting my point here.

All of this I wanted to tell Raphael as he moped in the dungeon. But I couldn't. Not yet.

It still wasn't my time to intervene…

5

Too exhausted to sleep, too numb to fear his own death, it finally occurred to Raphael to wonder about the events that had brought him to the dungeon.

Why had Juliana betrayed him? Earlier that morning, they had locked eyes, he was sure. Yet she claimed otherwise.

Perhaps she truly did not remember his face. Her beauty had enchanted him so fully that he could close his eyes and count each lovely strand of hair upon her head. Yet his feelings for her, of course, did not mean she could say the same for him.

But wait!

He had balanced outside her window in his jester's costume. Surely—even forgetting his face—she would remember his colors, or at the very least the jester's crown that had dangled about his face. And too, she had slammed the window shutters—proving she had definitely seen him outside.

Raphael frowned into the darkness at these realizations.

There could be no doubt, he told himself, that she should recall their brief meeting.

She had lied.

But why? Was she a part of the assassin's attempt?

Raphael thought further. Who had stolen his clothes? Who had placed them in the stable to make it look as though he was going to escape with a horse? Why had the stablemaster lied?

Raphael gnawed at his lower lip in doubt. He was a jester, after all. And among jesters, perhaps the most skilled. He could juggle, balance, throw knives, tumble, and somersault like few others in the kingdom. But thinking? This was strange and unaccustomed, especially when all his questions seemed to be such puzzles. He much preferred action over thought.

Like the action that had sent him after the assassin…the action that had sent him into this dungeon…the action that would lead to the horrible death of his family…

Raphael commanded himself to direct his thoughts back to the morning. Regrets would not help his family now.

Even in his pain and sorrow, Raphael laughed aloud at *that* thought. Chained and facing torture and then death, was there *any* way he could help his family?

He lapsed back into self-pity.

Minutes—was it hours?—later, cold water on the back of his neck startled him. He had nodded to sleep, and the next drop of water had missed his skull and landed squarely on the back of his neck.

He shook his head to wake himself. If the rats attacked...

Raphael took deep breaths.

He thought of Clement VI above, sleeping comfortably.

Then another thought.

How long might Clement VI remain safe?

Raphael knew he hadn't tried to kill Clement VI, but no one else knew that but the assassin himself. Would the assassin not try again? If Clement VI were killed, what then? Would all others see the jester as innocent, his claims of seeing that assassin finally proven true?

Perhaps, Raphael told himself, if he not been executed by then. At least his family might be granted life should the true assassin show himself.

Unless...

Raphael groaned.

Unless it was believed that whoever had placed silver in the saddlebag had merely hired another. Then on the death of Clement VI Raphael's family might be tortured as extra revenge.

If Raphael could have loosened his hands from the chains, he would have buried his head between them in utter hopelessness. He who preferred action over thought could do nothing except think thoughts of fear. He was powerless to do anything but await his own torture and death.

Another scuffle reached his ears.

Ha, Raphael thought, *who cares now about rats?* Let them chew my ears. Let them tear a hole in my neck and drink blood.

It all matters so little when pain and death will arrive soon anyway. It all matters so little when my family will die within the month.

A scuffle again. This one, however, stronger than the first. A man's shoes?

Raphael strained his eyes, but in the darkness saw only the deepest of black.

Another scuffle. A light clanking of metal against metal.

Keys?

Raphael was now fully awake.

He could sense the presence of another in the dungeon chamber, hinted by air moving across his face when air had been heavy and still. It was another sound—so slight as to be barely heard—scuffle of leather on stone.

He felt his scalp prickle.

If this were the jailer, he would be carrying a candle.

What could this mean?

A rough whisper, so close by that his heart almost jumped from his chest broke the silence.

"Call out softly."

For a moment, Raphael hesitated. Then he realized he was being a fool. One who approached with such stealth was also one who hid from the master of the dungeon. An enemy of the enemy, then, must be a friend.

"Here," Raphael whispered. It came out as a croak. "I am here."

Moments later, a hand brushed across his face.

Raphael fought the urge to scream. The hand trailed across his head, then shoulders. Another hand joined it as it searched out his arms, then the chains on his arms.

No words were spoken. It seemed as if it were an angel reaching for him, invisible in the darkness. But no angel would smell of stale sweat like this and have breath worse than rotted potatoes.

The hands fumbled with a key. Only briefly. The clasps fell away.

"Find your leg chains," the voice whispered. The man's breath washed over him as vapors from a sewer. Raphael did not complain, not when a key was pressed into one of his hands. "Release the clasps quietly."

Within heartbeats, Raphael was free. He had set each chain down with the utmost care, afraid that iron on stone might bring guards at full run.

Raphael stood. "I am ready," he whispered.

"Follow then," came the reply, barely heard. "Those who wait for you cannot wait long."

6

Juliana of Normandy stared out her window. Deep shadow covered the courtyard immediately below her, for the height of the palace had blocked the sun from as early as midafternoon.

She stood motionless and continued her unfocused stare, hardly aware as evening shadows began to spill over the rooftops on the far side of the palace.

He sits in chains, she thought again and again, *Raphael sits in chains because of me.* While her face was serene, Juliana churned with worry and fear inside. Despite the need to put Raphael in chains, she hated her memories of the look of frozen horror and disbelief on his face as she had condemned him to torture and death by denying their brief early morning meeting.

And, to be sure, the early morning meeting had been brief.

Juliana was still surprised at herself for having closed the window so harshly on Raphael. Normally she did little without carefully considering the action itself, what might follow from the action, and even what might follow after what might follow. Why then had she reacted so swiftly that morning?

This was not a question for Juliana to treat lightly. She treated no question lightly, especially any regarding herself. Others might fool themselves—she had seen in royal courts women so large and ugly they could hardly be recognized as women, yet who placed jewelry on their fingers and necks and convinced themselves of their great beauty. She had seen men who believed themselves to be pious and full of faith, yet who had little hesitation in kicking aside a crippled beggar. No, always Juliana wanted to know herself well and would search for and accept truth, even if the search or the truth was painful.

Why had she reacted so swiftly? As she watched twilight deepen, Juliana finally found her answer. She'd been angered at losing grip on her emotions. To see Raphael—magnificent and tall at the balcony—had brought a strange rush of joy and bewilderment, almost like a wave crashing over her. She could still feel those unfamiliar emotions as she recalled the morning.

She wished she could have lingered to gaze into his face and enjoy the wonderful sensation that arrived with seeing his open smile and the laughter dancing in his eyes. Why, even after slamming the window shut, she had opened the window again almost immediately, but by then it had been too late. Raphael had already begun to run from her balcony, crouching on the stone beam with balance and speed any cat might envy.

The rest had happened all too quickly.

Raphael throwing the juggling pin. The assassin turning the crossbow on him, then surrendering it before escape. The arrival of the soldiers. Then the knock on her door that had led to her audience with Clement VI, one of the most powerful men in all of Europe. And shortly after had come the threat which had forced her to deny she had ever seen Raphael.

Deny seeing him or find yourself dead. He will die anyway, and your efforts to help him will only bring your own death too.

Alfred, the captain of the guard, had whispered that threat as they walked together up the winding stairs through the Tower of Angels to the pope's study. This from the captain of the guard? He of broken teeth and a massive scarred face that showed sufficient fierceness to cause children nightmares?

Deny your meeting.

Minute by minute, Juliana divided her thoughts between anguish for Raphael and concern for where events might take him.

———————

Darkness had almost descended on Avignon when there was another knock on her door.

"Yes?" she said. Here in the guest's quarters, she had no reason to bar the door. "Enter. The door is not locked."

Without leaving her position at the window, she turned to greet her visitor.

"M'lady." It was a priest. "I have been instructed to deliver to you the name you trust."

"Yes?" Juliana whispered.

"Reynold." He watched her carefully. "I hope it satisfies you, for that is all I was given."

Juliana nodded. "You can be trusted. You have a message for me?"

"One has taken the key and entered the dungeon."

"That is all?" Juliana asked.

The priest nodded and bowed respect before backing out of the room.

It was enough of a message. Although the messenger had no idea of what he had delivered, she did, and she hurried to ready herself.

It had happened quicker than expected.

Already it might be too late for her to save the life of the jester.

7

Juliana shivered in the night air. She stood hidden in tall bushes at the north edge of the palace grounds, the highest point of Avignon, where the gardens ended with almost sheer cliffs down to the Rhone River. She had found the gardens and then slipped into the foliage, expecting them to arrive any minute.

If she had guessed wrong, the jester was dead.

Her serene face showed none of her fear.

Instead, she forced herself to show outward signs of patience. Among the bushes, she ignored the branch tips that tugged against her hair as they shifted with the wind. She kept her chin straight and looked ahead over the river.

Stars and the strong light of a full moon shimmered on the water, giving it a deceptive calm. Juliana knew better than to believe the flat surface of the water meant any degree of safety. Here in Avignon, the Rhone was swollen from dozens of rivers that entered upstream. Few rivers in the entire kingdom were mightier, and she had been warned early on that too many peasants, unable to swim, drowned each year from tumbling into the waters from bridges or shore.

Another minute passed.

She counted arches far below on the Pont St. Bénézet, the legendary huge stone bridge of Avignon that crossed to an island in the Rhone, then continued arch after arch over the island to the far banks of the river's deep swiftness. Of the 26 arches along the bridge, she was able to see only six before the ghostly pale stonework disappeared in the darkness.

Save for the occasional splash of water as the river surged against the bridge's foundation, little other noise reached her ears. This high and this far north of the town and palace, she was in complete isolation.

Her first warning of visitors was a grunt, the sound of a large man stumbling in the shadows of the gardens. The voice that followed made her tingle with recognition.

"Monsieur, are you certain we travel in the right direction? Here there is no way out except by flying like a bird. I know the palace grounds well and have yet to discover a path down the cliffs."

Raphael. His words were good-natured and gave no indication that he suspected his approaching death.

"And who is it that waits for me, monsieur?" Raphael asked. "Surely this far from the dungeon you can finally tell me."

"Not yet."

"Your name, monsieur? You can now tell me that?"

"Demigius," the large man said with impatience. "Now hold your tongue, jester. Is not the rescue in itself enough?"

"For which you have my gratitude, Demigius," Raphael replied. They were barely more than ten steps away from her. Juliana saw them as indistinct shapes moving slowly. "I wish, however—"

"You will see shortly enough."

There was a slight pause. She could hear the rustle of leaves against their bodies as they pushed through the garden.

"Monsieur," Raphael urged. "Watch for that—"

"Ummph," the large man said as he bumped his head into a low branch.

Raphael chuckled. "Perhaps I should lead. I do know the grounds. If you would tell me where you wished to go…"

Demigius grumbled low curses, and Raphael held his silence.

Juliana found herself breathing in shallow gasps. She could not afford to be found yet. The thought of what might happen if she failed added to her nervousness. Earlier she had condemned Raphael to death and torture; now she could not let him die.

They passed by her without seeing her among the tall bushes. She waited a few seconds and then stepped out to follow.

The two in front of her reached the edge of the cliffs. They followed along the edge to a point where the land jutted out over the sheer drop. The large man stopped.

"Monsieur," Raphael said, "I do not mean to show disrespect, but unless we have wings…"

"Yes," the large man said with cold softness. "It would serve you best if you did."

"Monsieur?"

Juliana moved closer. She saw the larger shadow raise his arm.

"Monsieur!" Raphael blurted as he saw it too. The sword, held high, its gleaming steel reflected by moonlight. He stepped backward away from the sword and onto the narrow point of land. To his left and to his right, only night air. And behind him, only three steps of safety before he would plunge to certain death on the rocks far below.

"Monsieur…"

"I could have killed you in the dungeon," Demigius said. His voice was flat, as if he were merely commenting on the weather. "But then I would have had to carry you here, and I am far too lazy for that."

Raphael tried a hesitant step forward. The man slashed his sword, a viscious cut that narrowly missed Raphael's chest. The swoosh of torn air carried clearly to Juliana. She had never felt such fear before. Fear for Raphael. Fear for what she must do.

The man kept his sword ready to swing again. Raphael did not move. He had no chance to duck past the man to the safety of the garden.

"I…I do not understand," Raphael said. "Why this trouble to…to…"

"End your life?" The continued flatness of the man's voice added to Juliana's fear. He was about to murder Raphael, yet treated it no differently than if he were cutting carrots for soup. "Jester, there are those who do not want to see you questioned. They much prefer that you die while attempting escape."

"Who?" Raphael said. "Who wishes that I die? And why?"

"I find your questions tedious. All that matters is your body be found on the rocks tomorrow in daylight." Demigius jabbed at Raphael with his sword. Raphael took an unwanted step backward. Two more steps and indeed he would be among the realm of angels.

Juliana reached into her cloak for the tiny weapon she had taken from her room. She forced herself to move out from the shadows that protected her.

"Good evening," she called with a cheerfulness she did not feel. "As I walked through the garden, I heard voices and…"

She stopped, as if seeing the sword for the first time. "What is this?"

Demigius turned slightly, able to keep Raphael out on the ledge and able to watch Juliana.

"Woman," Demigius grunted, "it would serve you well to walk away."

Raphael said nothing. His eyes were on the sword and any opportunity to dive past the man.

"Walk away?" she asked. "First convince me you mean the jester no harm."

"You recognize him?" Demigius sighed. "Woman, you have just brought your own death upon yourself."

8

"Run!" Raphael cried to Juliana, hoarse with desperation. "He will not leave me to chase you. Run now!"

Demigius danced a stutter step of hesitation, realizing that he could not attack both Raphael and Juliana at once.

"Run!" Raphael urged again as Juliana had not moved. "Escape!"

Juliana ignored his plea. She brought her right hand to her mouth and stepped toward Demigius. Darkness hid the short piece of narrow copper tube curled in her fist and aimed at the killer's throat.

"You dare fight me?" Demigius challenged her approach with a sneer. "A mere woman?"

Raphael edged toward Demigius, something that Juliana noted with a surge of warm gratitude. *He is willing to attack unarmed*, she thought, *because he believes me to be in danger*.

Demigius caught the motion out of the corner of his eye. He spun and slashed viciously at Raphael, who barely dodged the sword's blade with a backward jump.

"Bah," Demigius said with contempt as he turned his attention again to Juliana. "You both die."

Juliana drew breath but did not reply. She needed air in her lungs for another reason. One step closer and almost within range of the killer's sword, she blew hard, forcing a burst of air through the copper tube.

An instant later, Demigius slapped the side of his neck.

"What child's play is this?" he said. He pulled at his skin and answered his own question with a laugh. "A dart?"

He leered with joy, a horrible grimace in the moon's light, and then laughed again. "I quake with fear at such a weapon."

He waved his sword at Juliana. "When I finish with him, you die next. No matter how far you try to run."

With lazy confidence, he turned his back on her and faced Raphael. He jabbed the air in front of the jester.

Raphael inched backward.

"Ho!" Demigius said. "This has been so troublesome I will now delight to see you fall."

Another jab.

Another backward step by Raphael. One more half step and he would hurtle to his death on the rocks far below.

Juliana watched in confusion. *Surely the potion would take effect. Not even a man as big as Demigius could stand against the weapon she'd been given, a dart poisoned by an extract of herbs and roots.*

Demigius faked another jab. Raphael flinched, almost slipping on the edge of the crumbling rock.

"Woman, have you run yet?" Demigius taunted without looking back at Juliana. "Or do you wish to witness his death?"

Raphael's eyes were riveted on the sword blade. A part of Juliana's mind observed that in his final moments before death, Raphael did not beg or cry.

The other part of her mind, however, was forcing her into thoughts of action. Juliana contained herself no longer. She rushed forward to slam herself into the killer's back.

He heard the movement of her feet and with speed incredible for a man of his bulk, twisted and used his free hand to grab her hair. He spun with her and allowed her momentum to carry her past him into Raphael's arms.

For a moment, they both tottered at the cliff's edge. Only Raphael's strength kept them from disappearing into the darkness of the night air. They stood together, briefly in each other's arms, and then found their balance and faced Demigius.

"This is rich," Demigius chortled. He waved his sword at both of them. "You die together. I need not chase a quarrelsome woman through the garden."

Raphael stepped in front of Juliana, an act of useless defiance.

Juliana's heart raced in disbelief. *Had the potion aged and lost all power?*

A sudden gurgle from the killer finally told her otherwise. "What...strangeness...is...this..."

His voice trailed into weakness, and he lurched toward them. Demigius dropped to his knees at their feet then fell to his side. The sword tumbled from his fingers and clattered on the rocks.

Raphael snatched up the sword and stood above the huge man, ready to swing downward, as if he could not believe such good fortune. Juliana let herself breathe again and moved past both of them away from the cliff's edge to the safety of the garden.

"Jester," she called softly. "He will not rise soon. I promise you."

Raphael lifted his eyes from Demigius. "The dart?"

She nodded. "A potion."

Raphael backed away from the fallen man, reluctant to accept what his eyes and Juliana's words were telling him. Even at her side, he kept glancing at Demigius.

"Is he dead?" Raphael asked.

"No," she told him. "A deep sleep. It will leave him with an aching head."

"I thank you, then, m'lady," he said gravely. "Had you not gone for a moonlit stroll—"

He stopped. And stared into her face. "A moonlit stroll? In the remotest part of the garden?" His voice hardened. "Armed with a mysterious weapon?"

He stepped back from her.

"What is it?" Juliana whispered. His smile had turned to suspicion.

"Too much strange has happened in this day. Now I am to believe it was coincidence that brought you here?"

Juliana shook her head. "You think not?"

"No." Bitterness entered his accusation. "Had you but spoken earlier in the pope's presence, it would have cleared my name. My family's name. But in front of Clement VI, you condemned me to death. Along with my father, mother, and two sisters."

Juliana said nothing, but not for lack of words. Reply after reply raced through her mind. All the things she might say about why she was here on this night, about why she'd been brought here to Avignon.

Raphael took her silence as a lack of concern. "I was a fool to hope for more. What now? A dart for me too?" He swept his arm in a circle that took in most of the darkness of the garden beyond them. "Or have you saved me for a worse fate?"

This she could answer. "No. You are free."

He snorted a laugh of resignation. "Free? Only until my empty dungeon cell is discovered and every soldier in the land hunts for me. I shall be no better than a fleeing dog."

"Perhaps. Perhaps not." She studied Raphael intently, remembering how he had stepped in front of her to protect her from the sword of Demigius, determined to delay her death as long as possible. In his anger now, he was magnificent. The wave of confused joy and bewilderment from their first brief meeting hit her again. If only she could tell him what she knew. Instead she would have to hide behind a mask of cool indifference.

"Find your way to the first arch of the stone bridge," she said. "There you will discover a rowboat tied to the bank. Let the river take you downstream to the town of Tarascon. At the Church of Sainte Marthe, ask for Father Sebastian. He will hide you until this matter has ended."

Raphael shook his head. "You betrayed me once. Why should I believe you now?"

"Because you must." Juliana tried to keep her voice calm.

"What is your involvement in this? How did you know I would be led from the dungeon to the garden at this hour? Who placed the boat there?" Raphael stopped for breath from his rapid questions. "And why? Why all of this? Why did you betray me in the first place?"

Juliana looked at the ground.

In a flash, Raphael was upon her. He clenched his hand around her throat and tightened his fingers slightly. "Tell me. Or die."

She stared him in the eyes, their faces so close together she could feel the heat of his breath. She did not speak.

He dropped his hand. "Go. It shames me to think that I would even threaten you."

"You will follow my directions?"

"I will stand here until this Demigius awakes. Then I will threaten *him* with death for the answers I need."

"No," she pleaded. Reynold had made it clear. This jester's part had already been played; he must be gone before the rest might unfold.

"No?" Raphael asked.

The answer to his question came from elsewhere. Shouts from the direction of the palace broke the quiet of the night. Then came the sound to chill any fugitive—the baying of hounds.

"You have no time!" she said. "Your safety lies in escape. Take the boat."

Raphael ignored her. He was already moving toward Demigius. He spared no roughness as he turned the fallen man to pull his rough-hewn coat from him.

Juliana understood immediately. Disguise. The jester needed to cover his dirt-smeared court costume.

Moonlight showed the skin of his upper body a gleam of ghost white as Raphael stripped off his vest and jester's shirt. Juliana turned her head in modesty, and when he spoke again, he was almost at her side, covered by the coat he had stolen from Demigius.

"Drag my clothing behind you as you go," Raphael told her. "The scent will confuse the hounds into following you. You will do that?"

"Yes. Gladly," she said.

He leaned forward.

Before she knew what was happening, he had taken her hand in his and had gently kissed it.

"Whoever you are," he said. "You did save my life just now, even though you earlier condemned it. For that, you have my gratitude."

That is how he left her. With the warmth on the back of her hand where he had softly kissed. And with a deep sadness. She had sent him away. His part in this was now finished, and she would never see him again.

9

How far to Tarascon?

Raphael had been as close as Beaucaire, the town directly across from Tarascon on the other bank of the Rhone River. Beaucaire, while without a castle as famed as the one that guarded Tarascon, had something much more important to a young jester—the renowned July fair.

Despite his situation in the rowboat, Raphael almost smiled. The July fair, with its merchants, trained dogs, monkeys, bearded women, dwarfs, lion tamers. All were there to please the vast crowds, who thronged in such great numbers that many were forced to sleep in docked boats at night. The previous summer, Raphael had competed there against acrobats and jugglers who toured the rest of Europe. There he had begun to dream of leaving the quiet courts of Avignon. He had not once imagined fleeing for his life would take him toward Beaucaire, to take refuge in its enemy town across the waters, Tarascon.

How far to finally get there?

Last summer Raphael had traveled by land to Beaucaire, more than a half day's journey through the hills. Perhaps 15 miles. Here on the river, surely the journey would end sooner. The speed of the swirling black waters beneath the rowboat's hull dizzied him with fear.

A jester could juggle, walk a tightrope, throw knives. But swim?

Raphael clung to the edge of the boat, careful not to quickly shift his weight on the occasions he needed to row the oars. He felt as if he floated on a leaf, the boat was so small and unbalanced, the river so powerful.

How far to Tarascon?

He had already drifted an hour and had not enjoyed a single minute. When clouds curtained the moon, the river became even more sinister, the shore a menacing hulk of darkness. Yet when the clouds parted to let the moon bounce white off the waters, he realized anew the frailness of his boat on the mighty Rhone. During the precious few moments he forgot those fears, his mind would return to the events that had put him into the rowboat.

It had been only the previous dawn when he had first seen the assassin on the rooftop. Since then he had been sentenced to death, rescued to face another death, saved, and sent fleeing. He felt like an actor flung into a play, as if he had been put unawares among the minstrels and storytellers who all knew where the ballad began and ended.

Others, he thought with sudden anger, *knew the parts they played, and why. Juliana. Demigius. The assassin. Almost as if it all had been planned…*

Until that moment in the rowboat, Raphael had not once considered the strangeness of the first event that had led him into this trouble. His mind had churned with fear for his own life, his family's lives. Anger at Juliana's betrayal had consumed him. Bewilderment at the stablemaster's lie about the silver coins and clothing and purchased horse had added to the confusion. *Others knew the parts they played, and why. Juliana. Demigius. The assassin. Almost as if it all had been planned…*

Raphael wanted the boat to stop rocking in the currents so that he could concentrate on where his thoughts were leading. Jesters delight in action—logic and thinking took fierce concentration.

He ignored the lurching of the boat as the current swept him along, for in his mind he was on the rooftop again, running across the beam, seeing in his mind the events that led to his capture.

Yes…the assassin *had* acted strangely. He had deliberately fired the crossbow bolt *over* the pope and then set the crossbow down before fleeing. And…

Raphael frowned at a new thought.

The assassin had addressed him by name! Yet how could he have known his name? Raphael was certain they had not met each other before.

Could this man know Raphael by reputation? Doubtful. The dark-haired stranger was neither part of the royal court nor a servant. Not likely, then, one outside the papal palace should know of Raphael, let alone recognize him.

And if Raphael believed someone unseen and unknown had thrown him into this story, it might give reason too for why Demigius had been paid to lead him to his death. And reason for Juliana's timely appearance.

Perhaps five minutes passed as Raphael gnawed at those thoughts. Five minutes as the tiny boat tossed on the currents. Five minutes as the shoreline slid past. Five minutes until Raphael grinned in triumph at the moon.

He was not a thinker, and yet he had been able to come to a conclusion he could accept.

Yes, he could believe a master storyteller had begun all of this, writing parts for each of the players. That, at least, gave him an opponent to fight, even if the opponent had no face or name at this point. That, at least, let him take action instead of fleeing helplessly.

With new determination, he began to row toward shore. He would find this master storyteller. But first, Raphael told himself, he needed to arrange his own death.

10

Raphael stood upon a sharp-edged boulder and looked down on the small broken boat with satisfaction. The moon's glow—all the clouds had finally blown clear of the cold night sky—showed the boat in a pool of water where the river eddied at the base of that boulder.

It had taken Raphael a half hour of steady battering with fist-sized rocks to finally punch a splintered gap in the hull of the boat. It now lay upside down, the slime of the hull above the surface of the water, and the hole obvious even in the dim light of moon and stars.

Raphael had no doubt the boat would be discovered soon. His pounding of rock against wood had brought forth a curious audience—a herd of cows that had wandered closer to stare as they chewed their cuds. Cows meant farmers. And farmers meant someone would be along the river here in the next day or two. And that someone would turn the boat over to discover the jester's cap trapped beneath.

The way word moved through the countryside, it would take less than a day for it to be known in Avignon that the jester had drowned trying to escape. This might fool the master storyteller into relaxing his search for Raphael; it might not. But at least Raphael had taken counteraction, something that had already cheered him considerably.

He did not know who the master storyteller was. Nor why the events had been thrust upon him, the story written around him. To this point it mattered little, for simply this action of arranging the boat to make it appear he had drowned had let Raphael feel he had taken a tiny portion of control over the confusing events that had brought him here.

It also gave him a chance for purposeful action. It was a small chance, to be sure, and Raphael knew well that he had nothing but the clothes on his back and his guess that a master storyteller did exist.

Yet while Raphael had been pounding the boat's hull, he had let his mind ponder further. With what little he did know for certain, perhaps he could begin to unravel *how* the events had been arranged. Those threads might very well lead him to the mysterious person who had arranged to have Raphael falsely accused of treason and at the same time imposed the penalty of death on his family.

The prospect of action filled Raphael with enough hope that he did not mind, an hour later, the need to seek sleep in a hay pile several miles inland from the river.

He told himself that he would simply doze until dawn.

But exhausted as he was, sleep did not come easily.

Raphael burrowed into the hay as deep as he could, shifting and squirming like a restless baby. Yet whenever he laid his weight fully into the hay, he felt as if he were lying on small rocks.

Not until just before dawn did Raphael discover the reason for his discomfort. He truly had been sleeping on small hard objects—pieces of silver sewn into the lining of the coat he had taken from Demigius.

11

Silver?

Raphael hardly dared to trust what his fingers told him. At the bottom edge of the coat, he could feel objects sewn into a fold of the cloth—objects small, flat, circular, and hard.

Silver?

Earlier, during his shivering walk from the Rhone River inland, Raphael had puzzled again and again on how he might return unnoticed to Avignon. After all, no matter how dirty and ragged his clothes had become, passersby would note that he wore jester's tights on his legs. He'd wondered if somehow he might be able to barter with a tailor for regular trousers to let him blend in with the crowds. Yet what did he have to barter?

He had even considered as desperate an act as ambushing an unwary traveler and stealing his trousers to hide his jester's colors.

Even had he been able to solve the first problem, Raphael had wondered too how he might pay for food or lodging over the next days in Avignon. He could entertain passersby with his juggling and acrobats to collect coins, but if he did that, he might as well have trumpets and banners proclaim his entrance into Avignon.

But silver? Could this truly be silver in the lining of the coat?

Covered with coarse grass clinging to his hair and clothes, Raphael rose from the pile of hay and fumbled with the coat. At regular intervals along the bottom edge of the coat he felt the solid round outlines of a coin...then another...and another... until he had counted seven.

Seven silver coins? A half year's wages!

Raphael brought the bottom of the coat up to his mouth and used his teeth to snip a strand of thread. With trembling fingers, he pulled at the thread until he had loosened enough to gain grip on the fold of cloth that wrapped the first object he hoped and prayed truly was a piece of silver.

Yes!

Raphael grinned at the coin in the center of his palm.

Silver!

He brought the bottom of the coat up to his mouth again to snip the next thread, then paused, mouth half open.

Why not leave the rest of the silver hidden in the coat? It had taken him hours to discover the coins, and he had been wearing the coat. How much more difficult for anyone else to discover the wealth he now carried? It would be much safer for him not to have the jingle of coin obvious on him as he moved through the crowds of Avignon.

Satisfied at his decision and what he'd found, Raphael finally brushed the grass off himself.

He'd almost been thrown to his death from a cliff, he'd endured the terror of floating down the Rhone, he'd walked several hours in the chill of the night, and he'd barely slept any in this pile of hay. Yet now as he brushed himself clean, he whistled. He had money and hope, while yesterday he'd had nothing but the fear of torture and death for himself and his family.

With the sun bright above the horizon, the future was now indeed something to be faced with considerable more cheer than he could have expected...

Raphael let his whistled tune trail away.

What good did this newfound wealth do if he could not spend it? For unless he got rid of his colorful tights, any shopkeeper would see them and pass along word of a young jester seeking new clothes, especially in the face of whatever rumors of his death might arise from the discovery of the overturned boat.

Raphael groaned. His plans were getting complicated. What he would give for the simpler days when all he need worry about was how many balls he could juggle, how far to walk the tightrope, how many standing flips it would take to bring a smile from the patrons of the court.

Raphael sat back and pondered his new dilemma. Could he approach a peasant's hut and offer to purchase a set of clothing?

No, it was unlikely that any poor peasant had the luxury of owning a second set of clothing he could sell. Even if there were trousers available for purchase, talk of a young jester wandering from hut to hut in search of clothing would reach Avignon as quickly, if not more quickly, than news of the broken boat with the jester's cap.

A set of wrinkles entirely unfamiliar to Raphael's face furrowed his brow as he sat back against the pile of hay, deep in thought, the single silver coin clutched in his hand.

How *could* he find trousers to replace his jester's colors?

Half an hour later, when the sun was hot enough to rouse flies and bring ants forth from the ground, Raphael grinned at the solution that had taken him so long to reach.

All he needed to do was find a hog wallow.

Frankly, I was as confused as Raphael about what was going on.

Our Father, of course, knew the answers. But it is not His job to pass everything He knows onto angels. Nor do we expect it. Our trust in Him is sufficient, something that would make life easier on you if you would do the same.

All I knew was that I was to stay with Raphael.

It didn't mean, however, that I couldn't think for myself. Angels have had thousands of years of dealing with humans and observing you very closely without your knowledge of our presence, so I was prepared to make some pretty good guesses about what's going on.

What I did know was that Raphael was innocent of the charges of attempting to assassinate the pope. Because of this, I knew that someone had gone to great effort to make him look guilty.

Instead of wondering who had gone to the effort, I began to ask *why* someone would go to the effort.

And to that end, the answer was simple.

When humans lie to other humans, hurt other humans, or kill other humans, it's usually for power. (This includes money, since money is simply another form of power among humans.)

That meant someone had done all this to gain power.

All I needed to do was discover what power the assassination attempt involved, and it would point me to the person wanting that power.

So that was the big question.

What power or money could be gained by having the world believe an obscure jester was determined to kill the pope, the one man in the entire civilized world with the most power of all?

I felt much better when I had simplified Raphael's problem to that one question.

Of course, it hadn't led me to an answer.

But at least I knew the question.

And sometimes, having the right question is all you need.

I could afford to be patient.

As long as Raphael was still alive..

12

"Good afternoon, mademoiselle. I hope you will not mind this interruption."

Juliana lifted her eyes from the book in her hands. She'd been so absorbed in the words that she had barely realized the servant girl had entered her room. "Not at all. You are welcome here anytime."

The servant girl smiled shyly. The smile brought warmth to her thin face. She carried a jug of warm water for Juliana's wash basin. "I can see now why you spend little time with the rest of the travelers from England."

At first, Juliana did not understand. Then she glanced down at the open book.

"Oh, this," Juliana said. She closed the book, careful that the heavy pages did not wrinkle. "The pope's library contains writings from all across the known world. I thought it would be a terrible waste not to enjoy such an opportunity."

The servant girl poured the water in the basin. "How do words on a page speak to you?" She paused, then spoke quickly. "I would not normally ask, but you seem so kind and I've always wondered."

Juliana realized this girl was almost afraid. They were the same age, but the servant girl was treating her as if she were a queen.

And Juliana knew why.

For Juliana and for those around her who had been raised as she had, the ability to read was assumed, taken for granted. It took a situation like this to remind Juliana that usually only royalty and the most learned of the church were taught the special gift of reading. To peasants and servants, the power of books was frightening.

Juliana opened the book again. "Come closer," she said. "I'll try to show you."

Juliana pointed at a word. Looping lines of the letters hand scripted so beautifully on the page spelled out *cognito*. "Each mark or letter gives a different sound," Juliana said. "All the sounds together make the word."

Juliana pronounced it aloud for the girl as she ran her finger slowly beneath the word. "Cog-nee-toe."

"Cognito?" The girl laughed. "I've never heard such a word."

Again, Juliana had to pause and remind herself how different her world and how she'd been raised. Often, she didn't realize when her thoughts switched from one language to another.

"Latin," Juliana explained. "The language you hear the priests use in mass. *Cognito* means to be aware."

"Why a book in a language nobody understands?" the girl asked. "And who first made that language if only the priests speak it?"

Juliana looked at the servant girl. She looked hard, as if seeing her for the first time. The girl's eyes were bright with intelligence, her shoulders straight with pride. She truly did want to know. And curiosity was too precious, lost too easily with age. Juliana would answer her questions with patience.

"Latin is a language that all scholars and diplomats understand," Juliana replied. "Germans can write letters to Italians. Italians to the French. All of them use Latin as a common language."

The girl nodded.

"Latin began with the Romans," Juliana said. "Centuries ago. It spread with them as they conquered the world."

"Romans?"

Juliana smiled. She enjoyed being around someone with such a thirst for knowledge.

"Romans," Juliana repeated. "The greatest empire in history. They had water that ran into their houses—aqueducts. They had slaves to take care of every need. Many of the ruins you see in this countryside remain from when they ruled southern France."

The servant girl sat, mouth open, eagerly taking in each word.

Juliana closed the book again. She closed her eyes and recalled the lessons in history that she'd absorbed in her childhood. But where to begin when this girl knew so little of the world?

Half an hour later, Juliana finished.

"I cannot thank you enough, mademoiselle." The girl frowned. "Your wash water. It's now cold."

Juliana shrugged. "It's still wet, is it not?"

The servant girl grinned. "You *are* different. Some of the ladies I served would wish me whipped."

Juliana could not help but grin too. "What is your name?"

"Aliena."

They shared a friendly silence until Juliana spoke as casually as she could. Perhaps she could learn something in return about a matter much closer to her heart than ancient Rome.

"You have heard, I suppose, of the jester named Raphael?" Juliana asked.

Aliena nodded. "I cannot believe he is guilty."

"No? You knew him?" Juliana was glad to see that Aliena saw nothing unusual in her offhand questions, gladder still to see Aliena's eyes sparkle at the chance to share what she knew.

"The most skilled among jesters. He once climbed a tower and stood in the wind and juggled five balls," Aliena said. "On another day, he invited a girl to sit on his shoulders as he walked both of them across a strung rope."

Juliana nodded encouragement, much as Aliena had nodded during their discussion on Rome.

"Raphael was a great favorite among us," Aliena said. "When he smiled and looked into your eyes, it made your knees tremble."

Juliana felt an unfamiliar emotion. Jealousy, she realized. She bit the inside of her cheek in sudden anger at being so irrational and weak.

"He...he had someone special?" she finally asked.

"No," Aliena laughed. "Though we all tried. Some more than others. Some more than once." Her laugh sobered quickly. "And to think that now he is hunted not by servant girls but by the pope's guards."

"As one strange to this land," Juliana said, "I have followed the story with interest. How could he have first escaped the dungeon stronghold?"

"It *is* beyond belief," Aliena agreed. "Had you ever met Raphael, however, you might not express such surprise. Few jesters could equal him."

"People say had he not escaped, word of his attempt to kill the pope would never have reached our ears." Juliana was glad at this moment that the high officials of the pope's court had released so little information that her own involvement in condemning Raphael had been kept secret.

"Who knows the ways of the rich and powerful," Aliena said. Then blushed. "I meant no insult, mademoiselle."

"None taken." Juliana needed to keep Aliena at ease. "You need not assume that because I come from England that I am either rich or powerful." She smiled continued encouragement. "So you think this jester is innocent?"

"If you knew Raphael, you would know he could not have done this. Raphael tamed mice and kept them as pets. He fed pigeons from his window."

"There *is* the letter they found in his room," Juliana countered. "The letter instructing him to kill Clement VI. And the silver hidden beneath his bed as payment."

For the first time since speaking of Raphael, Aliena's certainty wavered. "Yes. That letter cannot be denied." Her face became sad. "Worse, I've heard it means his death. Poor Raphael."

Juliana fought a sudden chill. "Death? Surely if he is innocent it will be proved at his trial. An explanation for the letter, perhaps. A witness to vouch for him."

Aliena shook her head. "You have not heard?"

"No," Juliana said. And she had not. She had gladly embraced books as a means to occupy her attention over the last day, an escape from her worries and constant thoughts of Raphael. Until Aliena, there had been no one she trusted enough to even ask the simplest questions about Raphael.

"He will never reach a trial. The merchants of Avignon have posted a reward," Aliena said. "Even the best of Raphael's friends might be tempted to slit his throat."

"I...I...do not understand."

"Two pounds of gold have been offered by the wealthy men of business in Avignon," Aliena said. "Whether he is returned with or without his head, the reward for Raphael's capture is two pounds of gold coin."

13

"Answers?" Clement VI frowned, an intimidating sight from a man dressed in robes worth two months of wages. "I thought you understood what we put at risk to meet."

"I understand too well," Juliana said, "but I needed to see you."

Juliana would not be discouraged. The thought of gold in exchange for Raphael's head in a burlap sack had tormented her for hours. A simple answer from this man, and she could rest in peace.

They stood in the pope's chamber, more secluded even than the pope's study. Large foliages of vines and oak leaves were painted on the walls, with birds and squirrels painted on a blue background. They seemed to bring the room to life. The windows were decorated with bird cages, the floor covered with ornamental tiles. Truly a breathtaking room, worthy of the mightiest man in all of Europe.

Juliana had no eye for these details. She wanted instead to be reassured.

"We share one word," Juliana said. "*Reynold*. Without that word, I would not trust you. And with that word, you have certain obligations to me."

"That is why I am here." Clement VI was facing away from her. "I will help as I can."

"I only have one question and it concerns the jester. Can you give me assurance that he safely arrived in Tarascon?"

Clement VI turned and studied her face. "No other questions?"

"The reward of gold offered for his head causes me fear," Juliana explained. "I merely wish to know the jester is safely away from Avignon. We had arranged to keep him safe with your priest. Surely you know if he has arrived."

"I have a goddaughter your age," Clement VI said, the expression on his face gentle. "I would do my utmost to help her avoid pain and anguish."

He lifted his hand, as if to brush hair away from Juliana's forehead. Then stopped. "In the same way, I would wish to spare you."

"What is it?" Juliana felt more alarm at this sudden tenderness than she had at his frown.

"You should not take the guilt upon yourself," Clement VI said. "You are not to blame."

"I do not understand." But Juliana was afraid she did.

"I do understand," Clement VI said. His face sagged with weariness. "And I wish I did not."

"Raphael did not escape?" Juliana asked. "He is already captured?"

Clement VI shook his head. "Far worse. Drowned."

———————

Juliana returned to her chambers, fell across her bed, and mourned Raphael's death alone in silence. The pope's tale of the jester's cap found in an overturned boat deeply troubled her. Despite the pope's advice otherwise, Juliana did feel she was to blame for Raphael's death. The depth of her feelings of sorrow amazed her; until meeting Raphael, she had been convinced that logic and pure thought could always triumph over the emotions that swayed the weak. Now she was discovering that her heart *was* stronger than her mind.

She continued to mourn as the sky outside her window darkened with the beginning of a clear cold spring night. Then, as the deep purple became a black that glittered with stars, she heard a scraping on her balcony.

She wrapped herself in her robe and moved toward the window.

A half step later, she froze.

Her window was opening.

Her room was already dim, and the dark fabric of her robe made her almost invisible as she stepped aside to hide in the shadows of the drapes.

Backing through the open window, a monster stepped into her room.

A lesser woman would have screamed, for what little light shone through the drapes showed the figure to have rough, almost scaly skin. Its eyes gleamed from a face cracked and distorted into inhuman features.

And the stench!

The foulness of a sewer filled the room. Juliana imagined long dead corpses, flesh hanging from bones.

The monster straightened.

Juliana clenched her teeth.

Her childhood had not been without training in matters of defense. There was a point on a man's neck where the pressure of two fingertips would render him helpless, force him in a dead faint within seconds. Monster or not, she would not stand helpless and await its intentions.

Juliana stepped away from the drapes. She reached for the monster's neck.

Somehow, though, it detected her movement. It whirled, slapping away her hand. In another swift motion, it clasped her other wrist.

Briefly, they stood there. Locked. Juliana strained to pull her wrist free, then push it free. She could not budge against the monster's strength. She swung again at the monster's face with her free hand. The monster blocked that blow easily.

More seconds of silence, until a low laugh bubbled from the monster.

"M'lady, your appearance is deceptive. Who would think that such beauty hides such fierceness."

She gasped. *Raphael!*

Immediate anger washed over her surprise. Irrational anger that he had caused her such sorrow with news of his death.

"How dare you!" she blurted. "And to sneak in like a thief!"

"Shall I ask for an escort through the palace halls?" Raphael's voice lost its laughter, as if sudden anger took him as well. "Had you spoken truth earlier to the pope, I would not be in this situation."

They both realized he was still holding her wrists. It was an awkward moment, simply because with that realization, he continued to hold her close and she did not pull away.

Heartbeats ticked by. Finally, he dropped her hands.

She stared defiance at him.

"Call for guards, if you wish," he said quietly. "However, along with my death, you risk your own life. Consider that not a threat, but a promise."

"You would kill me, jester?"

"With regret." Raphael paused, his response piercing his own heart. "The lives of my parents and sisters are at stake. It drives me to such desperation."

"We will talk," Juliana said, "but not because I fear your threat. I have my own questions. Talk, I presume, is the reason for your visit."

Raphael nodded.

Juliana wrinkled her nose. "Is it your habit to call on ladies dressed in this manner and smelling so?"

"There is little safety in wearing jester's colors." He rubbed at his face. "I have spent the last day and a half hidden in the countryside. My disguise is the mud of a hog wallow, the only thing I could find that would hide both my jester's colors and my face should I be seen from a distance. Believe me, I find it as offensive as you do."

"Hidden in the countryside? I had heard you drowned."

"Excellent," he replied.

"More than you know. There is also a price on your head. Two pounds of gold. Believed dead, you may not be hunted."

Instead of shock or outrage, Raphael nodded thoughtfully. "Two pounds of gold? That's ten times the reward for even the most infamous criminals. The storyteller shows desperation."

"Storyteller?"

"Storyteller," Raphael said firmly. "And that is the reason I am here. You see—"

A knock at Juliana's door echoed over his whispered words.

Raphael jolted to rigid attention. "Are you expecting someone?" he asked softly.

"No."

"I cannot hide in here."

"Not unless my visitor has nostrils covered with garlic. Unseen or not, your presence could not be ignored."

The knock was repeated.

Raphael pressed something hard and flat into Juliana's hand. "Purchase clothing for me," he said. "Meet me tomorrow at midnight. Beneath the same arch that held the rowboat."

"You trust me?"

"You freed me once. And I have nowhere else to turn."

Another urgent knock.

Raphael turned away from her. "Food too. Please bring me food. I have not eaten since leaving Avignon."

With those words, he left with a quickness and agility that amazed her.

She opened the door to discover Aliena with fresh water and towels. Juliana hardly remembered acknowledging Aliena or closing the door after her departure.

Raphael. Alive. Here in Avignon.

How could she help him without betraying him once more?

14

Again, Juliana found herself alone at night staring at the Rhone River. This night, however, her view was not from the cliffs of the palace gardens. She now stood beneath the massive stone arches of the Bridge Saint Benezet, the river within her reach. All she need do was stoop and she could trail her fingers in the water.

She shivered, not entirely from the cold air of midnight. Some of the shiver was fear; some of it was anticipation.

Would Raphael be here as he had promised? All of last night and the following day had passed. Could he have remained hidden that long?

Juliana assured herself that word of the jester's capture surely would have reached her. Especially through Aliena. Their

friendship was growing stronger with each hour of shared conversation, and Juliana had made sure the servant spent as much
time as possible on nearby duties.

A click of stone against stone interrupted her thoughts. She
strained her eyes but saw nothing in the shadows of the great
bridge. The bank that led to the river was flat and grassy, and
the dim starlight showed no approaching figure. She told herself that the click had been a splash of water.

Five minutes passed. She set down the sack that held clothes
and food for Raphael.

Church bells tolled midnight.

Another five minutes.

Juliana walked a tight, nervous circle. The full moon that
had aided her a few evenings earlier had shrunk to a half circle,
but it still provided some light. She looked hard in all directions as she paced.

Twice she imagined strange noises, but twice she saw so little
that she was able to convince herself that she was alone.

The strain of waiting and not knowing became worse.

It suddenly occurred to her that perhaps her concern should
be not for his safety, but for her own. She was alone, after all,
outside of the town walls of Avignon, a difficult situation to
explain to palace officials, who expected their guests to behave
as guests. Worse, she had little protection against passersby with
unkindly intentions. And she could expect any passersby at this
time of night to carry unkindly intentions.

She began to imagine what might happen if a band of cut-
throat thieves came by. Not only did she have food and

clothing—well worth stealing—but she also carried the leftover money from her purchases for Raphael.

Bandits could easily surround her here, dispatch her with brutality, then throw her lifeless body into the river.

She shuddered at the thought. And if she were dead, how then could she fulfill the purpose of her visit here to Avignon?

Another strange noise. This one a whispered softness, as if a bat had winged past her head. She began to turn to search for the noise, and a hand gripped her shoulder.

Without thought, she whirled and drove her fist into her attacker. Her knuckles sunk deep into his stomach, and the figure fell to his knees.

She raised her foot to kick.

"No…ugh…more." The figure raised its hands in plea.

"Raphael?"

"I'm not certain," came the groan. "I need to collect my senses."

"Raphael! You nearly caused my death of fright."

He clutched his stomach and moaned. "Well, apparently you were wanting to cause my death by blows."

"Well, if you wouldn't have…" Juliana stopped, puzzled. "Where did you come from, anyway?"

On his knees, Raphael pointed above her. "Rope," he managed to croak.

She looked above her to see a darker shadow, a straight thin line that reached from the top of the arch to below the height of her waist.

"There's a ledge below the top of the bridge," Raphael explained in slow, pained words. "It seemed the best way to observe whether you were alone." He tried to chuckle. "When I lowered the rope, it almost hit your head. I had to wait until you moved before I could lower myself."

"Did you have to be so dramatic?" Even as she asked, Juliana was wondering why she was changing her admiration to scorn.

"Is there..." he coughed for breath, "...two pounds of gold as reward for *your* head?"

She nodded understanding.

Raphael slowly wobbled to his feet. Juliana caught the stench of the dried hog wallow mud in the evening breeze.

He groaned again.

Juliana tried not to giggle, but she didn't succeed.

"I find little humor in this." He staggered a few times. "It seems you bring me nothing but grief."

"Grief. I have clothes and food. Some would show gratitude to one who brings such to a wanted criminal."

He groaned again, but she suspected this one was for effect. "Food? Until a few moments ago, I had great hunger. Now, my stomach protests the prospect of eating."

Juliana was able to see by his grin in the pale gray of the moonlight that he was only kidding.

He stepped closer and she gave him the bag, pinching her nose with the fingers of her free hand to avoid the smell of the mud.

He noticed her movement and his grin widened. "I've become accustomed to my own stench," he said. "Still, it will feel good to discard the jester's colors. Were I not so afraid of drowning in the river's flow, I would ask for the privacy to bathe this very minute." He gave an apologetic shrug. "Stones swim better than I do."

"Perhaps a bath later," Juliana felt herself blushing and smiling all at once.

"Then I shall stand aside as I attack this food."

"Downwind, please," she teased.

He chuckled. The sound of it warmed her and also filled her with dread. She would have to betray him yet again, to save his life. He would never know or understand why. How could she hope to have his laughter ever warm her again?

It took him what seemed like seconds to devour a whole roasted chicken. He sucked dry a water-filled wineskin then peered into the sack and fumbled for more provisions.

"Don't eat it all now," she warned. "What will you have for tomorrow?"

"Only questions," he said. Still, she noticed, he heeded her advice and set the sack on the ground.

"Yes, questions," she said coolly. She feared the loss of dignity that might come if he knew how he affected her. Aloofness seemed the best way to handle the situation. "It was the purpose of our meeting."

"Questions." Raphael's voice lost its warmth to match hers. "Who told you to expect me in the garden? The same one who arranged for the boat to wait for me here?"

"I cannot answer." Much as she wished she could tell more, the levels of duty were clear to Juliana. First, she had a duty to her faith in God. Second, to her upbringing and the traditions of her Normandy family and its obligations to Clement VI. After that, if possible, she would help this jester.

"Cannot? Or will not?" Raphael's tone was accusing.

"Cannot," Juliana said after some thought. That much she *could* tell him.

"Cannot…" he mused. "That supports my belief that a storyteller is behind all of this."

"Storyteller? Last evening you had said the same. What of a storyteller?"

"You tell me," Raphael said.

"I cannot," she told him.

"Why did you betray me during our audience with the pope?"

She shook her head.

"You *did* see the assassin on the rooftop."

She could not ignore his pleading, as if he were afraid for his sanity. "Yes," she said after much inner debate. "I did see him."

"But you said otherwise to Clement VI. What can that mean?"

"I wish I was permitted to answer."

"Who denies you permission?" Raphael asked.

"I cannot say."

"This is useless," he said in sudden disgust. "You merely answer in circles." He lifted the sack. "I thank you for the provisions. And the clothing. Now, at least, I can ask questions of those who might answer."

He reached for the nearby rope.

"No," a deep voice reached them. "You will not ask questions."

Raphael whirled.

Three dark shadows advanced upon them.

15

"Betrayed again," he hissed at Juliana. "I was a fool to believe in you."

She did not deny his accusation.

Raphael did not pause to wait for any answer she might have. In a swift motion, he swung the sack upward and clamped his teeth on the edge of the material. Both hands free now, he grabbed the end of the rope and tucked it in the waistband of his tights. He jumped upward, reaching high with his hands. His fingers closed over the rope.

With incredible swiftness, he began to pull himself upward, hand over hand. Because the end of the rope was tucked in his tights, the loop of the rope followed him upward.

Two heartbeats later, he and the bottom loop of rope were out of reach of any man standing on the ground. Two heartbeats later, the three figures had reached Juliana.

She saw the uniforms of guards of the court and recognized the largest of the men.

"Alfred!" She put as much surprise into her voice as possible.

He ignored her as he watched the upward progress of the jester.

"He climbs faster than most men might descend," commented one of the guards.

"His reputation as king among jesters is well deserved," agreed Alfred. "Unfortunate, then, his attempt is doomed."

"Doomed?" Juliana echoed. She needed to act well, to play the role of a horrified spectator.

Alfred finally addressed her. "Doomed. Soldiers await him atop the bridge."

"But how—"

"You showed poor judgement to travel so freely in the markets of Avignon. Even the most dense could have figured out what you were doing. Buying clothing that was far too large for you and purchasing provisions when you could freely choose from the best of palace foods."

Above them, Raphael disappeared into the darkest shadows of the arch.

"And you paid little heed as you made your way here tonight," Alfred continued. "You were easy to follow."

Juliana clenched her fists as if furious with herself. *Now Raphael was safe. He would be captured by the pope's soldiers. The gold reward would be paid for his capture alive, not dead. And once within the pope's dungeon again, she would find a way to hide him once more.*

Raphael appeared briefly in the pale moonlight as he hugged the ledge that led to the outside of the arch. The rope was no longer tucked in the waistband of his tights. Two, three, four sliding steps and he was ready to scramble upward onto the top of the bridge.

"He *is* good," Alfred said softly. "Few men could have done that."

Raphael's grunt of effort reached down to them clearly. With a graceful leap, he hooked his fingers on the top edge of the stone, then pulled himself upward.

"Halt," came the clear, loud voice of one of the waiting soldiers.

Juliana could imagine the thoughts going through Raphael's mind. *Two pounds of gold for his head.* She wanted to cry out in anger and fear.

Instead, she did nothing. Already sick numbness filled her stomach. Nothing would ever convince him that she had not betrayed him yet again.

"Halt or die!" The commanding voice was clearer and louder in its insistence.

Juliana looked up again and saw nothing. She could only imagine what was taking place on the bridge as soliders advanced upon Raphael.

How could he fight against men armed with swords? Where could he run?

One of the guards beside Alfred pointed to the top of the bridge.

Juliana caught a glimpse of Raphael balanced briefly on the lip of the bridge, sack of clothing and food dangling from his left hand.

Then he leapt outward.

The image froze in her mind. His arms spread wide as if he were trying to fly. His body tumbling forward on itself in midair. The sack in his hand thrown back by rushing air.

It was a moment that stretched far too long. Then with a hard splash, he plunged into the deep, swirling waters.

The mighty current threw him into the arch of the bridge. He bounced back into the waters, rose briefly as he clawed for air, then disappeared.

Stones swim better, he had said. *I'd bathe were I not so afraid of the water.*

Alfred and the two guards ran to the edge of the bank.

"He can't swim!" Juliana shouted.

Raphael rose again, like a log spun upward as a plaything in the current.

Alfred and the guards ran along the edge of the bank.

They don't dare risk themselves, Juliana realized. Either they wish him dead, or they are as terrified of the river as Raphael.

As those thoughts were going through her head, Juliana found herself running toward the bank. Too surprised to question herself, she dove full length into the water.

Angel Blog

Angels rarely get credit where we deserve it.

Once, when Raphael was six years old, he climbed to the top of a church tower because he had it in his mind that he wanted to see the town like a bird. Unfortunately for him, he got more than a bird's-eye perspective. As a flock of pigeons scattered in panic at his appearance, one of them hit him squarely in the eye with a dropping. Raphael instinctively reached for his eye with his hands and lost his grip on the tile of the tower. He began to tumble down. Later, townspeople said it was a miracle that the end of his untucked shirt got caught in a crack. He dangled in the air, held only by his shirt, until a priest rescued him.

In a way, the townspeople were right. It *was* a miracle. What they didn't know was that *I'd* made sure the end of his shirt caught where it did. And I made sure the fabric of his shirt did not rip until he was rescued.

At nine, he first began to try to juggle pins. He chose ones that were too heavy. One hit him in the head and knocked him unconscious. His parents found him on his back in a mud puddle where he'd fallen. His head was propped up on one of the pins, like it had formed a pillow for him. If Raphael had fallen in any other position, he would have drowned, even though the puddle was barely four inches deep. Again, everyone agreed it was a miracle.

You probably won't find it a surprise when I tell you that, once again, I was simply doing my duty.

Another time, to test his heart, I approached him in the form of a crippled old man. He was eleven then and had just celebrated his birthday. He was walking through town, jingling coins in his pocket that had been a gift from a doting uncle.

As the crippled beggar, I told him that I was hungry.

It disappointed me when Raphael walked away. I said nothing. A few steps later, he turned and offered me one of his coins. I accepted it and he walked away.

But then he came back and gave all of them to me.

He had no idea how much I rejoiced—and how much more our Father rejoiced. And imagine Raphael's surprise when he rounded the next corner and found double the coins on the street, where it looked like they'd fallen from the purse of a wealthy merchant.

As you can see, I had entered Raphael's life on more occasions than he knew, and, because of directives from our Father, I'd been there every time he desperately needed help.

There, in the river below the bridge, was yet one more time.

I had no doubt he was about to drown unless something or someone could rescue him. Nothing in his own power could save him. The current of the black waters was too strong, the water too deep.

It was sweet and noble that Juliana had given into her impulse to dive in to save him. But it was also dumb. The river was far too powerful, and she was throwing her life away with his.

All she was able to do was reach him and hold his head above the water. She was unable to swim with him to safety.

The current bounced them around like little chips of wood, occasionally throwing them under, with both coming up again to gasp for air. They had only minutes left until the cold water dragged them down or until their legs caught on the branches of a water-logged tree waiting to drag them to their deaths.

I did not panic. Angels never panic. We trust our Father.

If this had been their time to die, I would have, of course, allowed it to happen. You humans sometimes see an early death as tragic, and we angels share the agony of that grief. But our grief is balanced by an understanding that death on earth does not end a person's existence. And we also understand that in our Father's presence time does not pass as it does on earth. With our Father, a day may seem like a thousand years, and a thousand years like a day. After you have stepped through the border to enter fully into His presence, a moment or two might pass for you while a generation passes on earth. And then, your loved ones step across the border to join you, so that on our side, you haven't had a chance to miss the ones you love. And those who missed you on earth suddenly understand, too, how temporary their grief was at your passing.

So if this was the time for the souls of Raphael and Juliana to leave behind the prison of their bodies, I would accept it.

I wasn't surprised, however, when I understood it was time to intervene.

You might call it a command from our Father, but it is much more. It is a joyous certainty, almost like a merging of thoughts. But I can explain it to you no better than trying to explain why gravity exists. You simply have to accept that it is there.

It was dark, and the waves of the river so powerful that I suppose I could have simply used the power given to me by our Father and pushed Raphael and Juliana both to shore, as if I were a giant unseen fish shoving them with my snout. I'm sure, had I chosen to do this, both would have believed later that it had been a fish, for humans struggle with the concept of angels as helpers.

But simply pushing them wouldn't have been a very elegant solution. And I hate to be accused of lacking in imagination. After all, when angels get together, we trade stories, and the better the rescue, the more entertaining to all the angels listening.

In a flash, I understood what would work.

There was a herd of horses near the river. And horses are great swimmers.

It wouldn't take much to panic them. Nor much to direct two of the strongest horses into a part of the river where the current would sweep Raphael and Juliana against their broad backs. Where both could grab the manes of the horses and hold on until the horses brought them back to shore.

So that's exactly what I did.

16

Alone and shivering wet, Raphael woke in darkness. He coughed violently at iron bands which seemed to squeeze his chest.

Then he remembered.

The river!

Desperate against all desperations on the bridge, he'd backed away from the soldiers and their advancing swords. That horrible moment as he tottered on the edge. Those heartbeats of fear as he fell, knowing as he plunged to the river that only a miracle could save him from death in the deep waters.

He'd fought hard against death, kicking upward in useless efforts to keep his head above water. The weight of his wet clothes had pulled him down again and again. And he'd kept a clenched grip on the burlap sack, knowing that without it, his life was worth little anyway.

He'd felt no more powerful than a helpless insect, sucked to certain doom, until the black of night had become a roaring in his ears, and the agony had finally faded to nothing as his struggles ended.

Now this? How was it that he was alive? Had he gone mad?

Without rising, Raphael coughed again. The pain in his chest racked him with each cough.

"Turn on your side," came a soft voice from the darkness.

He ignored the advice and searched for the voice. His eyes grew accustomed to the faint light of the moon, and he saw that he was lying in the shadows of a huge boulder. Lower down, and several hundred feet away, the black, deadly waters of the river reminded him of how horribly close he had come to dying.

Why had he not died?

"Turn on your side," the voice said again. "It is the water that you tried to breathe that gives you such pain."

He recognized the voice in the same instance that he dimly saw her in the shadows of a nearby boulder.

"Julia—" He coughed hard, sputtering as he tried to speak.

"Yes. Juliana," she answered. "The same."

He tried to speak, but the effort hurt him too badly.

"We are downstream from Avignon," she said. "Not too far. I dragged you up here to keep us hidden should the soldiers search for us."

"You! You dragged me here? You dove in?"

"Foolish of me," Juliana replied.

"Again!" Raphael still wheezed and choked out his words. "An insult!"

"No," she said. "I meant foolish of me because the river nearly drowned me too."

"So how is it we're not dead?"

"The strangest thing," she mused. "Horses. Suddenly appearing in front of me. I had you with one hand and was about to go under myself, when two great horses arrived. As if sent by God."

"I'm sure it was just coincidence," Raphael said. "It—"
Coughing seized him again.

"Turn on your side."

He did as directed. Raphael coughed again almost immediately, and he felt water rise within him. The pain of coughing weakened him so much that all he could do was turn his head and let the water fall from his mouth. When he coughed next, it hurt less and barely any water dribbled from the side of his mouth.

He stayed in that position, coughing and clearing his lungs. When it seemed that the bands of pain around his chest had eased, he struggled to sit.

That effort took all his energy.

Back against the boulder, he remained motionless for long minutes as he waited for the waves of nausea to subside. Slowly, much too slowly, he felt strength return. His shivering began anew, and he clenched his teeth to keep from chattering.

"Why?" he finally asked. He hugged his knees to warm himself.

"Why?" she repeated.

"Again you betrayed me. And again you saved me. Why?"

Juliana sighed. "It appears that I betrayed you because I did not know I had been followed. And..." She faltered. "And I saved you because I could not merely watch while you died."

"I suppose I must believe that, because here you are with me." Raphael had enough strength to manage a snort of mixed laughter and disgust. "The soldiers witnessed your attempt to save me. You realize that you now share whatever punishment awaits me."

Her answer was quiet. "I do."

Raphael sensed there was much more to her answer than those two simple words, but it was said with such sadness, that he was afraid to ask.

They shared silence.

Above the edge of the boulders, across the unprotected hill, a wind began to push at the grass and trees. Clouds, the first of the night, moved across the moon. The shadows of the rocks became invisible in the heightened darkness.

"Who are you?" Raphael finally asked. It was not a challenge. Not asked in anger or bitterness. It was almost a question of hopelessness, of someone so lost that he did not know where to turn.

She waited so long across from him in the darkness that he wondered if she had even heard. In his mind, he saw her as he had first seen her. The long raven hair. Eyes deeper blue than any sapphire. The softness of her face, the tilt of her chin, the mystery of her grace. In the darkness, he smiled sadly, even as he shivered. As much as he wanted to hold her and that mystery, he could not believe he would ever truly know her.

"Who are you?" he tried again with that same helpless wonder. "You appear when least expected. You take down large men with tiny darts. You triumph over the mighty Rhone, entering as boldly as any fish. You hold secrets of plots and assassins and your very presence makes my head light. So I'll ask again. Who are you?"

"Juliana of Normandy," she said above the sigh of the wind.

Before he could protest that he already knew that simple detail, she continued.

"I am a distant cousin to Clement VI," she went on. "As you may know, he was once the Abbot of Fecamp in Normandy. He, like me and all of my family, are intensely loyal to the French, although he must temper his loyalty by ensuring all under his rule are treated fairly."

"You serve him? Secretly?"

"Yes," she said.

"Why?"

A longer silence than the first, as if she were weighing in her mind what she might tell him. Raphael did not break that silence with impatient questions. He waited.

"Telling you completely would break a promise more important to me than my life. Can you accept that?"

"Yes," Raphael said, almost surprised that he truly meant it. Something in her voice had hinted at incredible agony—he did not desire to add to her sorrow.

Her next words startled him.

"Yet I will tell you as much as I can," she said.

17

"Explain first, though, where you got the silver coin you gave to me," Juliana said.

"Silver coin?"

"Jesters do not have the wealth of kings. Yet you gave me a silver coin as if it were nothing."

Raphael leaned forward, still huddled over his knees, but curious at the accusation behind her words.

"Are you saying it would be unusual for a jester to have a silver coin?"

"I am saying I want to trust you."

Raphael thought of the six remaining pieces of silver sewn in his jacket lining. "On the contrary, I need to trust *you* before I tell."

"Very well."

He expected her to continue, but the sound of the wind cutting across the hills replaced conversation. Several minutes passed before he realized that her "*very well*" meant just the opposite. She expected him to speak.

"You might recall that I took the jacket off Demigius back in the palace garden," Raphael told her.

In the dark, he could see her head lift as she brought her attention back to him.

"In the lining of his jacket," he continued, "I found pieces of silver. Perhaps his payment for leading me to death."

She said nothing.

Raphael removed the coat and threw it at her feet. Damp as the coat was, he discovered the night chill worsened without it.

"Feel for yourself," he said. "You must know that in the few days since then I had neither time nor opportunity nor skill to sew them into the lining myself."

Juliana stood. She scooped the coat into her hands but did not, as he expected, run her fingers along the bottom edges of the coat. Instead, she moved toward him and draped the coat over his back. The tenderness of her act and her trust in not searching for the silver touched him. Again he felt the strange mixture of sadness and joy to think of loving someone so mysterious.

She sat next to him.

"Raphael." Her voice was quiet. "The payment for killing the pope was found in your room. Along with the letter of instruction. You can't deny that."

"Not mine, I can assure you." He spoke solemnly. "Someone put those things there without my knowledge."

"You cannot blame me for wondering."

Raphael forgot the cold and the rawness of his throat from coughing. "I tell you! A master storyteller directs the events around me!"

Raphael explained the thoughts he'd had during his time in the rowboat. He did not explain, however, *how* he had decided to find the master storyteller.

"There is some truth in what you say," she agreed when he finished.

"But why?" Raphael asked. "That is the question which threatens to drive me mad. Why go to such lengths to involve me in an attempt to kill Clement VI?"

"Not you."

"Not me?" Raphael became indignant. "Not me? Who else do you suppose spent time in the dungeon? Who else nearly died at the cliff walls of the palace garden? Who now runs with the price of two pounds of gold on his head?"

She placed a hand on his arm to silence him. Her fingers were soft. Warm. She left her hand upon him.

"No, Raphael. It was not done to you. Rather, the politics and events make you a helpless pawn."

Suddenly, the comforting warmth of her hand on his arm felt like the burning of molten iron. He pulled his arm away at his sudden suspicions.

"How is it *you* know?"

She laughed softly at his reaction. "I am not part of the plot against you. Remember, I am sitting here beside you. Equally wet. Equally chilled. Were I against you, I would have watched you drown then returned to the comfort of my bed."

Raphael relaxed. He regretted his rash action, for now her hands were in her lap and he wished for the touch of her fingers on his arm.

"Then how is it you know?" His words were much gentler.

She took a moment to gather her thoughts. The clouds above them broke apart, their shadows fleeing as ghosts. In the new light of the moon, he could clearly see her eyes closed, the beauty of her face.

"This is," she began. Then stopped and cocked her head.

Raphael heard what she heard.

The baying of hounds.

He took her by the hand.

"I'll keep us safe," he promised. "In return, I want you to tell me what you can at the first opportunity."

18

"Last night," Raphael said, "you promised an explanation."

"You may recall we did have to escape the hounds." Juliana seemed to be in a more cheerful mood than anytime earlier. He thought he heard a smile in her words. Raphael, however, could not confirm his guess. Walking at her side and holding her arm to guide her steps, he could not see her face.

Even had he looked at her, he would have had difficulty seeing her smile. A shawl covered most of her face, a long coat most of her body. She walked bent and stooped as if she were an old lady, leaning on her cane with her other arm as she slowly moved down the uneven cobblestones on the streets of Avignon.

The streets were already crowded. Potters. Goldsmiths. Tailors. Wine merchants. Shoemakers. Butchers. All hawked their wares, most at top volume. Musicians danced to their own playing of flutes, a sight that brought an ache to Raphael's heart—he missed the joy of entertaining crowds with his own skills.

The shops, since few could read, were not marked with words painted on signs but with colorfully painted symbols. Stores were wedged together in long lines along the crooked streets, roofs so high and the street so narrow that even in mid-morning Raphael and Juliana walked in shadow.

It had taken them several hours since dawn to return to the town walls of Avignon. They'd watched the gates to see if soldiers waited to inspect the crowds that entered Avignon and had finally satisfied themselves that it was safe to join those crowds.

Once past the gates, Raphael had gone to an inn and waited for Juliana. She had hastened to purchase the shawl, coat, and cane for herself. She'd also gone to a tannery and bartered copper coins for some of the dye that tanners used to darken leather. Back at the small room rented at the inn, she had applied the dye to Raphael's blond hair.

As they now walked through the streets, Raphael in his rough clothing and with a small sack in his hand, appeared to be a kindly peasant farmer helping his elderly mother through the markets of Avignon. No peasant farmer with an elderly mother, however, would have flushed as Raphael did to remember his slumber the night before.

"You did fall asleep while I was talking," Juliana reminded him.

Indeed, exhausted as only a fugitive can be when death might arrive with any next heartbeat, he *had* fallen asleep as she spoke. He flushed to think of how he'd woken to discover Juliana curled beside him, an arm thrown over his chest to keep them both warm against the cold of the night. Yes, her closeness had been entirely pleasant. So pleasant that he almost wished he might fall again into the Rhone River some night soon.

He coughed to hide his embarrassment and quickly continued with his question. "How is it *you* know that great lengths were taken to make the attempt on the pope's life?"

She stopped, clutched his arm as if she had stumbled. "How far until we reach our destination?"

"At this pace? *I* may be old before we arrive."

"That allows me time then. I shall explain as we walk. In the noise of this crowd, there is little danger that unfriendly ears will overhear our conversation."

She clutched his arm closer to her. To any others, it would have seemed that the kindly peasant farmer was humoring his elderly mother with exaggerated attention. To Raphael, her closeness brought another flush to his face.

"How many people live in Avignon?" she asked.

"I haven't given it much thought," he said with a shrug. "Thousands upon thousands?"

"More," she replied. "And if you were to listen to the babble around us, you would hear the language of nearly every mother tongue in Europe. Avignon is the crossroads of all Christendom. Italy's largest banks are centered here. Architects and decorators from France. Men of letters and artists from every country known. Hundreds of administrators."

"Yes," Raphael said. "And so…?"

"Why are they here?" she demanded, with some impatience, as if the answer was obvious.

He hesitated.

"Why have the Italian banking centers moved here from Rome? Who has hired the artists? Whose wealth is attended by the administrators?"

"All because of the pope," Raphael said. "Clement VI."

"And before him?"

"I entertain crowds with feats of skill," Raphael said. "Why fill my head with unneeded historical nonsense?"

Her fingers tightened on his arm. "Nonsense? Matters of the mind are nonsense?"

Raphael was too stubborn to admit otherwise. "When I can strive to be the best juggler the courts have seen, I see no need to waste my time otherwise."

"Had you wasted your time otherwise," Juliana said sharply, "you would have known that for almost fifty years, Avignon has grown, and grown wealthy as the result of the decision of Clement V to move the papacy here away from Rome those fifty years ago."

Raphael attempted to shrug again, but her firm grip prevented him.

"And had you decided matters of the mind were important," she continued with the same impatience, "you might easily have realized that without the pope and his palace here, Avignon will no longer be the crossroads of all Christendom."

"Why would the pope leave?" Raphael was intrigued despite his stung pride.

"For one, the war that England has fought with France over the last dozens of years. Surely even you know that Edward III has long laid claim from England to the French throne. Surely even you know of the great battles in northern France less than ten years ago. Surely even you know that conquered towns like Calais are considered English strongholds in the heart of France."

"M'lady," Raphael said, "by the tone of your voice, you wish to do battle with me."

Juliana walked several halting steps in silence. When she spoke again, her voice no longer held anger. "Please forgive me. You and I will not battle."

She drew a breath. "King Edward in England wishes to continue war with France. He is deeply in debt to Italian bankers who have financed much of his war thus far. Italian bankers would love to see nothing better than the papacy return to Rome. If Edward rules France, and if the Italian bankers pressure Edward, will the papacy continue to enjoy its shelter here?"

Raphael understood she did not expect a reply. He continued to help her through the crowds of people around them. And he listened.

"No," she said. "Clement VI would be forced to move. Even without that, Clement VI also faces the same pressure to leave which every pope here has faced since Avignon was first established as the papal residency. While Avignon is well-placed in the center of Europe, Rome is the symbolic heart of the church. After all, the church grew from there. Saint Peter himself is buried there. As are many of the other great saints. Some of the feuds and disputes which first drove the popes away from Rome have ended. Exile here by the popes is no longer a political necessity."

"The pope leave Avignon and return to Rome?" Raphael spoke as he mused, so deep in thought that he stepped into a puddle and hardly flinched. "I had never considered it."

"It is not farfetched," Juliana said. "Anyone who pays attention to political matters finds it obvious."

Raphael kept his next thoughts to himself as he recalled strange words Clement VI had spoken to him during the brief audience. *There are some papal matters of great importance which are in delicate negotiations*, the pope had said. *It will do no good for word of an attempt on my life to reach certain ears.*

Could these delicate negotiations be related to a papal move from Avignon? And if so…

"There would be those who would oppose a papal move," Raphael said suddenly and with conviction. "Those whose wealth depends upon future prosperity of Avignon as the crossroads of all Christendom."

He heard Juliana chuckle. "For all your jester skills, I believe I may safely say that your mind is equally impressive. You are correct. A great many in Avignon have staked great wealth on the gamble that Avignon remains the home of the pope and his royal court."

Raphael again felt a flush of warmth. How was it that her praise could mean so much?

"How much at stake? Enough to suit their purpose very well if Clement VI were assassinated before he made a decision to take the papacy back to Rome." Juliana answered her own question before Raphael could utter a word. "Enough to threaten his successor with the same fate should the same decision be attempted."

"Has Clement VI made such a decision?"

"He nears it."

They had reached a crossroad. Wider. Filled with the traffic of horses and wagons instead of milling crowds of people. Raphael put his arm across Juliana's stooped shoulders to guide her safely along the side.

For a moment, she stiffened. Only for a moment. Then she relaxed and let him guide her along.

"There is more than wealth at stake," she said. "You may be frightened to hear how important it is that you and I succeed."

Raphael waited.

"If the pope is killed and it appears that Italy was behind it, then England finally has an excuse to declare war against Italy. The countries of Europe will be forced to choose sides. Either England or Italy."

"Why would England want war so badly against Italy?"

"Remember the enormous debt that the English king has to the Italian bankers."

Raphael nodded.

"If England is at war against Italy, it will have the perfect excuse not to honor the loans."

"What do I care about money matters?" Raphael asked.

"It is not the money. It is the prospect of war." She paused. "Think about it. What if all the countries in Europe become involved in a war that essentially covers the civilized world? Think of the hundreds of thousands who would be killed, the families that will grieve."

She shook her head. "Most of all, think about civilization itself. A war that big could very well put us back in the times when the Roman empire had collapsed. A new dark age would fall upon humankind."

She took his arm. "You and I, it appears, are the only ones who can prevent this. That's why I need your trust and your help."

19

Shadows, swarming flies, and the smell of warm, moist hay greeted them as they stepped into the stable.

"Remember," Raphael whispered, "you distract him. And as promised, I will not harm him at all."

Juliana nodded.

They moved ahead. A horse, haltered and tied to a rail, stamped nervousness.

They saw no other person.

"Strange," Raphael whispered, "this is mid-morning. No sign of him."

He strained his eyes to see in the dimness of the building. The roof was low. Piles of dirty straw covered the dirt floor. The only light came from small squares cut in the stone walls. He saw only two horses tethered, yet room for easily a dozen more.

He saw no sign of the stablemaster.

How can this be? Raphael felt the heaviness of dread in his stomach. His entire plan depended on finding the stablemaster. Someone had bribed the stablemaster to lie. Forcing the truth from him would be the first link in whatever chain would lead to the storyteller behind all of this.

To assure himself, Raphael hefted the small sack he carried in his hand. It held a small length of rope and a knife. He intended to bind the stablemaster and threaten his life for those crucial answers. Wherever those answers led, Raphael would follow.

None of this, however, would begin unless the stablemaster was here. And it would be risking much to return later, for Raphael was a marked man inside Avignon. He had to move quickly and move unpredictably. Not only did his life depend on this but his family's as well.

They reached the end of the stable. A small door led out behind to where more horses might enjoy sunshine in a small courtyard.

If the stablemaster were not outside…

Raphael pushed the door. It did not budge.

Strange.

He pushed again. Harder.

Behind him, the sound of heavy wood slamming into stone. The main doors into the stable had been shut.

Raphael turned to the new sound, Juliana with him.

With those doors at the front of the stable now closed, the inside of the stable grew even darker. Dust danced in the square beams of sunlight cast through the openings of the stone walls. Raphael could see only the outlines of an approaching figure in the deepened shadows.

Without thinking, he pushed Juliana behind him. Something about the figure's approach showed a certainty. A deadly intention.

"Who goes there?" Raphael called.

No answer.

Five more steps. The figure stepped through a shaft of sunlight.

Without hesitation, Raphael reached into his sack for his knife. That brief glimpse had shown him hair, dark and curling behind the ears, framing a narrow face and glittering eyes. The hooked nose. The cold smile of large white teeth. The same cruel face of a man who had aimed a crossbow at his heart from a rooftop. *The pope's assassin had reappeared.*

"No crossbow on this occasion?" Raphael asked. He wondered if his pounding heart was louder than his question. "You will not find me so helpless."

Silence, accept for the soft tread of footsteps across scattered straw.

Raphael crouched and held his knife in front of him. He had never before fought with a knife. But he was a jester. Fast hands. Sure eyes. A body trained to perform deeds of skill under the pressure of the watching eyes of large crowds. He would not die quietly. At the very least, he could attempt to save Juliana by surviving long enough to let her flee through the other door.

"It is him," Raphael hissed to Juliana, "the one who attempted to kill the pope!"

Raphael felt a surge of adrenaline. If he could beat this killer, he could ask questions. Questions to lead to the storyteller who had sent the assassin to kill the pope and now perhaps him.

A few more steps and Raphael could lunge forward with the knife.

Yet the assassin did not draw a weapon of his own.

Strangely, he brought his fist to his lips instead.

Raphael had seen such a movement before. He tried to recall where. It came to him the same moment he heard the puff of expelled breath.

In the garden…

He tried to react. *In the garden Juliana had toppled Demigius in the same—*

Too late. As he was throwing himself sideways, he felt a sharp stab of pain on his neck. He slapped at his skin and found a tiny dart.

"No," he moaned. "It cannot be."

He spun back to Juliana. "You? But how…"

"I'm sorry," she whispered. "I had no choice."

He tried to form more words, but his lips felt numb, his knees like collapsing hinges.

As he sagged forward, the dim shadows of the stable became the blackness of his worst nightmare.

Poor, poor Raphael.

Are you sensing sarcasm here instead of compassion?

He wasn't going to die there in the stable. How did I know? I'd been sent to protect him in the river. Although I would never presume to speak for our Father, it was logical for me to assume that I'd be sent again if his life were in real danger. Thus, I didn't have to waste any time feeling sorry for him.

But I was almost certain that he would wake up feeling sorry for himself. Hence, my sarcasm.

Let me burst a bubble for you.

Life is not supposed to be easy.

If it was supposed to be easy, your self-pity would be justified. If it was supposed to be easy, I'd understand when you humans walk around wringing your hands with a "woe is me" expression for the world to enjoy.

But life is difficult.

Here are three words for you: Get over it.

Not only is life difficult, but you should expect it to be a series of problems that continue and continue until you breathe your last breath on this earth.

Depressing?

Only if you expect that life is going to be easy.

But there's a wonderful paradox. As soon as you approach life with the attitude that it will be difficult, then life becomes much easier.

Because when you have the right expectations, you're not constantly disappointed.

After all, you don't step outside in a blizzard in a bathing suit, ready to apply suntan lotion and read a book beside the pool. No, you look outside, see the snow hitting the ground, and you dress according to what conditions you expect to face. Then, in a parka and boots, the weather is much easier to bear and you don't think twice about it once you're outside.

Faith is not meant to make your life easier.

Faith is meant to sustain you and help you understand there is a purpose to life on earth, a reason to persevere through any and all problems.

If I ever had the chance, I would try to tell this to Raphael.

In the meantime, I doubted he would be in a very good mood when he woke up...

❧◦❧

20

Raphael woke. Thirsty. Flies tickled his face as they crawled across his skin.

Raphael shook them loose and immediately regretted the sudden movement. His head throbbed, and he blinked his eyes into wakefulness.

He was still in the stable. Sitting in straw. Back to a wooden pole. His hands were cramped in an awkward position behind his back. It took several moments for him to realize his wrists were tied together.

Raphael groaned and fought to his feet. He tried to take a step forward. Pain stabbed through his shoulders. It took another several moments of struggle to understand that his wrists were bound behind the pole. He could sit and he could stand, but beyond that, no movement at all.

He groaned again. This time more at Juliana's betrayal than at his aching head and the tearing pain of his shoulders and arms.

The locked door. The absent stablemaster. The arrival of the assassin. It was all too perfect. He'd been led here to a trap, like a fly drawn by the honey of her sweetness. What a fool he'd been. The hour that she had taken to purchase her clothing and the tanner's dye *had* seemed too long. She must have used that time to arrange this trap.

Raphael told himself he should have listened to his first inner suspicions when he sat in the dungeon.

She was a puppet of the storyteller, an actor in one of his ballads.

She had betrayed him to the pope. Her excuses for that could easily have been lies, lies he accepted because he had wanted to, deceived so easily by his heart.

She had brought the soldiers to him beneath the bridge.

She had told the storyteller of his intentions to threaten the stablemaster. The trap would have been child's play for the storyteller, for if he had first bribed the stablemaster, he could have easily bribed the stablemaster again to be absent.

Why?

And why, in light of all of her betrayals, would Juliana take such efforts to keep him alive?

She could have let Demigius kill him in the gardens. She could have let him drown in the river. She could have had him killed here in the stable.

Instead, he was alive. Throbbing head. Cramped arms and shoulders. Bound to the pole behind him. But alive.

Why?

His jaw tightened in anger.

He would find out why. He would wring it from her neck, ignoring that beautiful face and finally twisting the truth from her. Then he would hunt down the storyteller and exact a payment of vengeance which would make death seem like a blessed relief.

But how to escape from the stable?

Raphael laughed a low, mean laugh.

For certain, she and the assassin had bound him to the pole. Yet they had forgotten he was Raphael, the finest jester in the land.

The pole was set only half a step away from the stone wall behind it.

Raphael knew exactly what he would do.

He would lie on his stomach. Yes, it would bring great pain to pull so hard at his wrists. But that same pain would also give him leverage to push at the stone wall with his feet.

Face down, he would slowly walk backwards up the wall, using the leverage of his wrists against the pole to hold him horizontal to the ground as he shuffled his way upward.

At the top, he would be able to slip his hands over the pole. No matter how hard he fell, he *would* land feet first. He was

Raphael the jester, now driven by ice cold anger, and nothing would stop him from escape.

Away from the pole, he would lie on his side, curled like a sleeping baby. He would slide his hands toward his feet, and contort and wiggle until he forced his bound wrists from behind his back to behind his legs. Few others could be so flexible, but he was Raphael the jester, swearing to take revenge on the woman he had once hoped to love.

With his hands behind his legs, he would sit, then pull one ankle through, then the other, so that his bound wrists were finally in front of him. A difficult task, but not impossible for a jester.

No matter how long it took, he would gnaw at the knots with his teeth until the rope loosened.

Once freed, he would hunt Juliana down like the despicable dog she was.

Raphael felt the anger build inside him. And savored it. It was an anger that would drive him to victory. At any cost.

Before evening dusk settled on Avignon, he was free.

21

Raphael stood in the shadows on the outer balcony of Juliana's room and waited. At his feet were the same rope and knife he had intended to use on the stablemaster.

Scaling the rooftops and darting along the ledges to bring him here had been a minor effort compared to the pain of working himself loose from the stable. He enjoyed the uncramped rest his wait afforded him.

While his body was at rest, however, his mind danced with thought after thought.

Much of Juliana's earlier conversations now made sense.

Knowledge of how near the pope was to making a decision to leave Avignon?

From the master storyteller.

Family and traditions and duty to France?

Serving the master storyteller.

He almost smacked the balcony rail in sudden fury.

And she had played him for a fool since the beginning.

Raphael froze, despite the anger that screamed inside him. The light of a candle inside her room told him that she had arrived.

Now, his fury demanded of himself. He would rush inside and hold the knife to her throat and get the truth from her lips.

Yet another part of the same anger—the cold, calculating icy rage—told him to wait. Patience would accomplish more than rash action. He could follow her until she met with the storyteller. As his puppet, surely she must meet him soon.

He crouched and held motionless.

A moment later, he felt overwhelming relief at his decision.

Another candle entered the room.

Who had joined her?

Juliana soon moved near the window to open the drapes.

Beside her stood the assassin, clearly lit by the candle he held.

Raphael hoped the shadow covered him completely. He forced himself to remain still, despite the conflicting urges inside him. One part wanted to join battle with the assassin. The other part wanted to flee.

He did nothing.

They looked out the window, but the glare of the candle-light in their own eyes made it impossible for either to see into the shadows of the balcony.

If either stepped to open the window...

Raphael held his breath.

They remained in the same spot and spoke in low voices to each other. Raphael heard nothing except a low murmur. Occasionally their voices rose, as if they were arguing without heat.

Raphael could only guess at how long the discussion continued. He only knew that if it didn't end soon, his thighs would burst from the strain of remaining in his crouch.

Finally, they turned away from the window.

Raphael followed the progress of the light of the candles as they opened the door and stepped out into the palace hallway again.

He smiled.

Two could be followed as easily as one.

22

Juliana lifted the heavy iron knocker and hesitated before she let it drop on the massive door in front of her. Once it fell, there would be no turning back.

She told herself that her worries were unnecessary.

Behind her stood ten of the staunchest soldiers from the pope's personal guard. And, of course, Reynold, who knew as much as any man alive about the ways to disable an opponent.

No, she had nothing to fear from the men inside this house on the outskirts of Avignon.

She told herself, too, that she had good reason for this attack. After all, she had seen the faces of the men as each had entered this house during the midnight hour. Dressed in rich velvets, wearing jewels that glittered in the light of their servants' oil lamps, these were definitely men of wealth, men of wealth who could only have sinister reasons for assembling this late at night in the remote corner of Avignon.

She let the knocker fall. And again. In her nervousness, the ponderous echoes seemed like thunder.

Without knowing it, she held her breath as she waited. Only when the view hole of the door slid open did she draw another breath.

"Go away," the voice on the other side of the door said.

Juliana could only see the man's eyes.

"I am here on the order of Pope Clement VI," she said.

The view hole slammed shut.

She smiled at the closed door. If it didn't open immediately, she'd know that the news had not been well received.

The door did not open.

She turned back to the soldiers and nodded.

They carried a battering ram, a long pole with handles on the side, so five men on each side could hold it horizontally. At her nod, they charged forward.

The door exploded under the impact of their driving legs.

Without pause, the soldiers dropped their battering ram, pulled free their swords, and dashed into the house.

Juliana and Reynold followed.

They found the soldiers in a large room in the center of the house. A fire crackled from the hearth nearby, throwing a dance of light across the men who were frozen in position in the chairs that lined the room.

The only other person standing, aside from the armed soldiers, was Alfred.

He stared, open mouthed, at Juliana.

"What is the meaning of this?" he demanded when he recovered his voice.

"Spare the drama," Juliana said. "You know better than I do the reasons you have to fear the wrath of Clement VI. These soldiers are here to arrest you. And the other men in this room."

Many of those velvet-covered men of wealth were obscenely fat. They stirred in their chairs but found difficulty in rising quickly.

"Arrest?"

"For treason," Juliana replied.

"Do you have proof?"

"Enough." Despite that answer, she felt misgivings. Alfred seemed too confident. "It will be brought forth at your trial."

"Ah," he said. "Along with your witness? Demigius the hired killer?"

His words hit her like blows.

He understood the reaction on her face. He smiled the smile of a cat toying with a crippled bird.

"I see you find it startling that I know of Demigius." He paused, enjoying the effect he had on her. "My pretty little fool. I sent him out hoping you would take him as bait. After all, how could I get you to appear here, tonight, at my convenience?"

Juliana sternly told herself to ignore the urge to back away from Alfred.

"Juliana, Juliana," Alfred continued, "don't you understand? It was obvious to me that Clement VI was trying to discover who was behind the threats against him. My difficulty was in an uncertainty of the identity of my enemy. Demigius, of course, was my way to find out."

He swept his arm around him to indicate the dozen or so men in their chairs. "Yes, these are the men you seek. Rich men of business, as you probably guessed, who would prefer Clement VI die to the alternative of seeing the papal court leave Avignon."

Muttering from several of the men greeted that remark.

Alfred scowled, a terrible enough sight that silence fell on the group.

"And yes," he said, "as you have guessed, I am in their hire. But if you think your arrival here is a surprise, you are wrong. *Dead* wrong."

Juliana felt more uncertainty. Could not Alfred see the soldiers, their swords drawn?

Alfred laughed, as if reading her thoughts. "Simply put, my pretty fool, I needed to find a way to get you into the open. My business friends here accomplished that."

"Alfred," one said in an angry voice, "this is…this is…"

"Shut your mouth," Alfred said.

"But—"

Alfred sighed. He turned from Juliana and directed his words to the men in the chairs. "We needed to discover our enemy. I sent Demigius forth, knowing he would be taken. I also knew the only loyalty that Demigius feels is toward silver. I'd told Demigius that we would be meeting here, tonight."

"You used us as bait!" another nearly shouted. "You cannot sacrifice us in this manner!"

"Sacrifice?" Alfred was unruffled. "Hardly."

"The soldiers!" This from the man nearest the fire. "We cannot fight!"

Alfred nodded. "Which is why you have me in your hire. I *can* fight. As can my own men."

Alfred nodded, his gaze past Juliana. "Now would suffice, gentlemen. Earn those fat bribes."

Even before she turned, Juliana knew she had lost. And when she faced the soldiers, her eyes confirmed the dread that filled her stomach.

Eight of the soldiers she had brought now surrounded Reynold and the other two soldiers.

"Very good," Alfred said. "You are not stupid enough to resist." He turned to Juliana. "I'll admit, it comes as surprise to me that it is you serving Clement VI. And I'll also admit it grieves me. For someone so young and beautiful should not have to die."

23

"You should count yourself fortunate that at present you are worth more alive than dead," Alfred sneered.

Juliana found little consolation in his words. She was tied up, lying in the back of a wagon. Reynold was equally helpless beside her. Both breathed heavily through flared nostrils; the soldiers had stuffed dirty cloths into their mouths as gags. Alfred stood above, ready to cover them both with a heavy blanket.

Alfred smiled. His face was little more than shadow, his broken teeth a pale gleam. "After all, I would be stupid to believe that you had not yet informed Clement VI of my identity. As hostages, you provide me the means to barter should the need arise."

He threw the blanket over Juliana and Reynold, sealing them from the moonlight and stars.

His laughter, however, reached her.

He pulled the top of the blanket back and leaned so close she had to wrinkle her nose against his putrid breath.

"Of course," he whispered, "tomorrow night the pope will die. A peaceful death in his sleep. But nonetheless, he will die." Alfred paused. "Then you will no longer be worth more alive than dead."

He flipped the blanket back over their faces.

The wagon lurched forward.

Juliana tried to guess its destination by the twists and turns, but she knew it was hopeless. The crooked streets of Avignon made such guesswork impossible.

And what difference would it make if she knew their destination? She held little hope of rescue. The drivers of the wagons were soldiers, those same handpicked men from the papal guard. Who would stop or challenge a guard in the colors of the papal uniform?

Juliana bit her tongue in frustration. How stupid not to foresee the possibility that guards would turn against her. Not only would she pay with her own life for her blunder, but with the life of Reynold as well. And worse, with the life of the pope.

She shuddered to think of the consequences of a successful assassination attempt on the pope.

She remembered her conversation with Raphael, how she had explained the politics and the possibility of war all across Europe. Her blunder would cost hundreds of thousands of lives, if not more. Children without mothers. Wives without husbands.

Another thought struck her at that remembered conversation.

Raphael!

Who would rescue him? She and Reynold had bribed the stablemaster to travel to Paris. No one would return to release Raphael for at least a week. He would be long dead of thirst by then—a horrible way to die.

Juliana realized with surprise that she grieved more for Raphael than for herself. She'd told herself again and again they could never be together. She'd told herself again and again to put him from her mind. Yet now, as she thought of him dying, she deeply grieved him and the loss of hope for his love.

All because of her stupidity.

The wooden wheels of the wagon groaned and clattered over the cobblestone, a noise in the quiet nighttime streets that hid the sound of Juliana's weeping.

Curiosity is essential to creativity.

True or not, you may be saying, *how does that statement relate to the story you are telling about this jester?*

But this is a great truth, especially for those of you who prefer to ignore the fact that humans have souls.

I offer both as pointers to the human soul.

Curiosity.

Creativity.

Look around the animal kingdom. You will find creatures that exhibit curiosity, but not for the sake of curiosity. Instinct compels them to be curious about their surroundings because their lives depend on that knowledge. Humans, however, are the only inhabitants of this world who are curious when it serves no practical purpose.

The same with creativity. You might try to argue, for example, that birds, like humans, express creative urges with their beautiful songs. But robins sing like robins; from generation to generation their melody, wonderful as it might be, does not change. Meadowlarks sing like meadowlarks and bluebirds like bluebirds. All of this is to our Father's glory.

Humans, on the other hand, are unique among all the inhabitants of our Father's world. Your creativity leads to amazing and varied works of art. Each generation is different from the next.

I argue, then, that the simple fact of your unique curiosity and creativity—you alone out of all the millions of species—should indicate very strongly to you that you have an invisible soul, a reflection of our Father, the ultimate Creator.

Should it surprise you, then, that we angels, also products of His creation, share those human traits?

Yes, this was a long-winded way of explaining that I, too, enjoy curiosity.

And now, I was truly, truly curious as to who Juliana was and what would happen to her.

I was not, however, her guardian, but Raphael's. If her life was in danger, I could not expect to be sent to intervene by our Father.

But Raphael, on the other hand...

24

At the base of the cliffs below the north end of the palace garden, Raphael shook his head no. He shook it violently, as if the harder he told himself no, the more he might convince himself to remain behind the bush that hid him from the boat.

He failed to persuade himself.

After all, he stood almost exactly where several nights earlier Demigius wanted to push him from the cliffs high above. Juliana had rescued him then. Even though she'd betrayed him twice since, he did owe her for his life.

Not only that, if he didn't find the master storyteller through her, he would forever remain a fugitive, his family doomed to execution because of it.

Yet why did it have to be the river?

He had followed Juliana and the hated assassin, she had called him "Reynold," to a house in the remote corner of Avignon. He had watched as the soldiers with them battered down the door. He had puzzled the meaning of this while he waited to see who might leave. Finally, he had stayed with the wagon that took Juliana and Reynold to the town gates nearest the river.

There, it had become more difficult. Armed only with the rope and knife he'd been carrying since the stable, Raphael could not hope to overpower the guards at the town gate. Instead, he managed to distract them with the age-old trick of heaving large rocks in the other direction then sprinting through the gate while they investigated the noise.

He'd nearly lost the wagon because the wheels were no longer rattling over cobblestone. He had only found it again because he'd heard the curses of one of the soldiers as they forced the horses to pull it through some mud near the river.

Then Raphael had crept close to discover a large boat moored to shore. He'd watched as the soldiers carried Juliana and Reynold onto the boat.

Raphael had expected the ropes which held the boat to shore to be loosened immediately. Instead, one soldier had departed with the wagon and horses. The other had moved into the boat and settled down for a wait.

As Raphael watched, he knew there would be no better time than now to take action. Obviously, the soldier expected someone else to arrive. Would it not be better to rush the boat before others joined this lone soldier?

Yet why did it have to be the river?

If Raphael fell overboard during the fight, certainly he would drown. And because it was the river, Raphael did not have the luxury of choosing to follow the boat should it leave.

No, he would have to act now.

Raphael shuddered. He feared very little. Heights were nothing. Running across something as narrow as a sagging rope was as easy as falling asleep. He could juggle five pins at once. But swim? It did not help that every time he closed his eyes he could feel it again—the black river closing over him and sucking him down to...

Stop!

He told himself it did no good to think of the possibility of his death. He told himself to remember that it was Juliana who had rescued him from the mighty Rhone. He told himself he had no choice but to risk those black waters.

The soldier had settled in the boat, sitting with his back against the bow. With the poor light of moon and stars, Raphael had an excellent chance to get close unobserved.

He crouched and stepped out from the bush. He had the rope wrapped around his waist, the knife in his hand.

Step by stealthy step, he approached the boat. It was far bigger than the rowboat which had first taken him down the river—this one could easily hold ten grown men. Its bow was high enough that Raphael knew the soldier inside would not see him. A single rope held the boat to shore, its bow pointed upstream toward Raphael.

The splashes of the river current masked any noise his feet might have made in the soft ground. He crept to within reach of the bow.

This was the moment to jump up, scramble over the bow, and overwhelm the soldier with surprise.

Raphael placed the blade of the knife flat and held it between his teeth. He needed both hands free to haul himself into the boat.

He took a breath and tensed.

"Halt!" The soldier's voice clearly broke the night air. "Who goes there?"

Raphael froze. *How could the soldier have—*

"Alfred, fool," another voice answered back. "And keep your voice down."

Alfred. The captain of the guards. Approaching from the down river side of the boat.

Raphael eased himself into the river to keep the boat between him and Alfred.

"Are all things ready?" Alfred asked, his voice ringing louder as he neared the boat.

"Yes, sire. Come on board and all that needs done is to cut the rope that holds us to shore."

"Excellent." Alfred was almost to the boat.

Raphael stepped farther into the river. Already the water swirled well above his knees, pulling at him with the power he knew all too well. Yet he had to keep the boat between him and Alfred.

He kept one hand on the rough wood of the boat's hull. He used that to guide him as he stepped deeper into the river. The water surged above his thighs—cold as ice, cold as death.

Now he was directly opposite shore, with the boat between him and Alfred.

The boat rocked. Alfred had boarded.

Raphael thought of his own rope wrapped around his waist. He had only one chance. The boat *must* have a hook or ring at the stern, for surely there would be times when it needed more than a bow rope to keep it moored.

He kept wading, torn between the urgency to rush and the need to prevent splashing or losing his balance. Each step was an agony of suspense.

"Don't delay, man," Alfred commanded. "Cut us loose."

"Yes, sire."

The boat moved up and down as the soldier clambered to reach the rope.

Raphael let the curve of the boat guide him to the stern. He reached up, praying that his hand would find—

Yes!

A large iron ring, screwed into the wood at the top of the back of the stern. He pulled an end of the rope loose from his waist and frantically threaded it through the ring. He was almost standing now, his head only inches below the top of the stern. He had to knot it quickly. Any second the boat would spin in the current and drift loose.

Without warning, the boat bumped back, nearly knocking him over.

The rope at the bow had been cut.

Raphael pulled hard on his knot. He had to trust that he'd tied it well enough to hold.

The boat turned in the current.

The soldier started to row.

Raphael ducked to hide. The water reached his chin. He let the rope slide through his hands, then wrapped the end around his wrist.

In moments, he was trailing the boat, almost like a fish tied to a heavy line. Far too quickly the boat reached mid-river. Raphael hung onto the rope, fought to keep his head above the water, and commanded himself not to think of the deep, dark water below him.

25

It didn't take long for Raphael to understand he had made a mistake.

He had first thought it would be possible to stay with the boat until it moored again. Indeed, he had congratulated himself on finding a clever way to stay with the boat.

However, to keep the knife in his teeth, he couldn't close his mouth. He found himself constantly gagging as he half choked against the water forced into his face. The river's coldness numbed him, and his hands became weaker from the strain of trying to maintain a hold on the slippery rope. Almost immediately, he realized he would be fortunate to last another mile of river.

How far did Alfred intend to take this boat?

Raphael had no way of guessing.

In short, he needed to take desperate measures.

He reached ahead with one hand. He clenched the rope until he was certain of a firm grip before he reached ahead with the other. He climbed forward, pulling himself against the heaviness of the water.

Raphael was thankful for the size of the boat, the sound of rushing water, and the darkness of the night. Pulling in this manner against a smaller boat would be easily felt by those inside. Instead, the larger boat towed his weight effortlessly, giving no warning of his presence. The sound of the water hid any of his splashes, and the night darkness kept him invisible as he approached the boat.

The true test would be in how quickly he could clamber into the boat. The water supported much of his weight. Once even halfway out, he would have to fight against not only his body weight but the weight of his water-soaked clothes.

He decided to try to ease his way up. If he could climb the last length of rope slowly, he would avoid rocking the boat. With luck, neither Alfred nor the soldier would notice his hands grip the top of the stern.

Raphael began to lift himself out of the water.

He gritted his teeth against the noise of water draining from his clothes into the river.

Slower, he told himself, *rise slower.*

The strain tore at his arms. His shoulders began to burn as he inched his way upward. Finally, he was able to hook the fingers of one hand over the top edge of the boat. Then the fingers of the other.

Would the slight silhouette of his knuckles be seen?

Raphael had to risk it, because unless he rested, he would not have the strength to pull himself into the boat.

The height of the stern was such that he now hung with most of his body out of the water, his feet trailing behind. He rested there, wanting to heave for breath but unable to open his mouth fully because of the knife in his teeth.

He could feel his fingers beginning to slip.

The fear of falling back into the river drove him to strength he did not know he had. With frantic effort, he pulled up, hard.

All the flips he'd ever practiced as a jester, all the times he trained by walking across the length of a rope stretched between two poles, all his hours of endless sweat had prepared him for this moment.

He was up, over, and rolling onto his feet in one rush of movement. Its total surprise stunned the soldier who sat on a high middle bench at the oars, facing the stern as he rowed.

Raphael moved on instinct, not even pausing to remove the knife from his teeth. He continued his forward motion and kicked the soldier in the jaw. The blow of his foot against solid bone jarred Raphael into staggering for balance. The soldier collapsed, flopping backward into the bow where Alfred stood overlooking the river ahead. Juliana and Reynold were tied and bound at Alfred's feet.

Alfred spun at the commotion.

The soldier groaned once, rolled to the side of the bow, then sagged into silence.

Alfred stared across the short distance to Raphael.

"What madness is this?"

Raphael reached for the knife between his teeth and hefted it in his right hand. He could only imagine how he appeared, an apparition rising from the waters.

"The madness is all yours," Raphael panted. "Whatever game it is you play, you may now consider it ended."

Alfred dropped his hand to his waist. Slowly, with supreme confidence, he withdrew his sword.

"Do I recognize the voice of the jester?" He laughed. "How amusing."

He stepped toward Raphael, waving his sword lazily.

Juliana and Reynold squirmed against their ropes. Backs against the curve of the bow, they saw clearly the drama in the center of the boat.

Raphael flinched and pressed backward toward the stern. What hope did he have with this small knife against a sword? Especially against a ruthless soldier who had fought his way to the top of the ranks of the papal guard?

Clouds broke open, letting moonlight fill the boat. Raphael saw that Juliana and Reynold had their hands bound in front.

He decided on a desperate gamble.

"I surrender," he told Alfred. "I did not expect you to be armed with a sword."

He bent and slowly placed the knife at his feet.

"Surrender? I had hoped for a fight. Your easy death will give me no pleasure at all."

Alfred took another step forward. He cut the air with his sword. The tip passed within a few feet of Raphael's midsection.

Now! The gamble!

Raphael kicked the knife ahead. It slid beneath the middle bench, directly between Juliana and Reynold.

Alfred, intent on his victim, missed the slight movement of Raphael's foot. He swiped again with his sword. This blow would have nicked Raphael's face had he not flung his head back.

Raphael danced away from the sword.

Another vicious swing.

Alfred laughed. "How much farther back can you go, jester?"

Raphael felt the stern press against his legs.

"So what is it, jester? Death by sword? Or death by drowning?"

Alfred set the point of his sword down and leaned on it as if it were a cane. His relaxed manner showed supreme confidence as he spoke. "Jester," he said, "the sword is quick but painful. Drowning, I'm told is peaceful, but much longer."

"Why?" Raphael said. Anything to keep Alfred talking. "Why this boat? Why all of this?"

Alfred laughed again. "How could a dim-witted jester understand my perfect schemings?"

"Those men at the house," Raphael said. "They've hired you to kill Clement VI."

"I was in the perfect position to do so, jester. For the gold I was offered, I could not refuse."

"Avignon men? Afraid to see Clement VI move the papal court to Rome?"

"What?" Alfred said with mock cheerfulness. "A jester who looks beyond jesting? I am impressed with your knowledge. And no, not Avignon men. English bankers."

"English bankers want the pope dead? I thought they wanted him to move to Rome."

"Of course they do." The boat rocked at a swell. Raphael fought for balance. Alfred, leaning on his sword and enjoying the cat and mouse game, barely swayed. "You see, jester, if it could *appear* as if Avignon men of business had killed the pope, quite naturally the next pope would find a safer city to live."

Raphael did not dare look beyond Alfred, did not dare hope. "So," Raphael guessed, "if Clement VI did not announce his decision to move to Rome, he would die."

"I knew yesterday that he had decided to stay," Alfred said. "The pope dies tomorrow." Alfred lifted his sword. "As for me, I will be safely gone."

Raphael held up his hand. "Amuse the jester, if you will. How can the pope die if you are gone?"

"An asp."

"A poisonous snake?"

"The pope returns from travels tomorrow. When he crawls into his bed tomorrow night, he'll discover that he does not sleep alone." A short mean laugh. "Or for long."

Alfred thrust his sword at Raphael. "Where will you take it, jester. Throat? Belly?"

"One last thing," Raphael said. "The assassination attempt that I stopped. If you were waiting for the pope's decision before trying to kill him, I don't understand…"

Alfred snorted. "No more questions, jester."

As he finished speaking, Alfred slashed at Raphael's face.

Raphael hopped up and backwards.

He balanced on the edge of the stern as only the jester could do.

The sword closed in on him, and he pushed off, still facing the boat.

He spread his arms wide, hoping, praying, that he'd find the trailing rope before the river pulled him down.

He kicked once. Twice. Water closed over his head. Darkness roared at him. Then his fingers brushed against the rough hemp of the rope. He grabbed hard, clawed his way to the surface.

Raphael coughed water, heaved in the blessed relief of cold night air. He shook his head free of water and looked upward.

Alfred was a black silhouette, outlined against night sky. His hands were on his hips as he looked downward into the water.

At Raphael's splashing, Alfred lifted his sword again.

"Ho, ho, jester, the rope will do you little good when it leaves the boat."

Just before Alfred could bring the sword down to slice through the rope, Raphael saw another silhouette. This one armed with only a knife.

With a swiftness that the jester could envy, the second silhouette grabbed Alfred's hair with one hand and brought the knife to Alfred's throat with the other.

"Slice that rope, soldier," came Reynold's voice, "and I slice your throat."

Is this the happy ending you wanted? Raphael alive, saved by Reynold at the last possible instant? Juliana alive? Justice about to be administered to the bad guy?

With those questions in mind, I submit once again that it takes willful blindness to ignore the invisible foundation that makes you human. Your soul.

If you did not have a soul, where would come your hope for justice, your natural understanding of what is good and what is evil? If our Father was not the Great Presence and the Great Light and the Great Good behind this universe, how would you be able to recognize there was any difference between good and evil?

A dog, for example, intelligent as it is compared to most other creatures around you, would never understand the events I've described, let alone care about the end result.

But you humans are clearly set apart from the rest of creation, and that awareness alone should alert you to a greater purpose for your species.

You may find satisfaction in discovering that Raphael and Juliana would survive this. You may find satisfaction in knowing that with the pope's assassination averted, so too was a war that might have devastated Europe. A war that would have involved all of the countries and their resources. A war that would have taken countless lives before our Father wanted those lives sent into His Presence. A war that would have set back the advance of civilization by centuries.

So, had I been sent to save Raphael long enough for him to change the course of civilization for the better?

Or had I been sent to ensure that he would live long enough to accept faith in our Father, so that when his life on earth did end, he would be received with joy among us?

Both, perhaps. Our Father knows best.

I knew, however, that it would be a pleasure to see him on our side of the border between life on earth and eternal life in the presence of our Father. I would delight in telling him about the times I saved him during childhood, as I would also delight in telling him about the night I sent the horses into the river, and of all the other occasions when our Father's invisible hand of love was upon him.

Yet whatever satisfaction you might have had in seeing his survival was a sadness of sorts for me.

I knew that my time with him had ended. Our Father no longer required me to remain as his guardian. Soon enough I, Pelagius, would be sent among you again to watch over another.

Yet I was still curious.

And our Father granted my wish to learn the rest of what I wanted to know about Juliana and her jester...

26

"I betrayed you three times and yet you trust me enough to meet in the garden?" Juliana found it difficult to keep her voice steady. At sunrise the next morn, she would depart from Avignon. There was much she wished to say to the jester.

Raphael nodded. "You have no further reason to betray me. The pope is alive. Alfred is in the dungeon."

"Had you not supplied me with the knife to cut Reynold free..." Juliana shuddered. Despite the bright sunshine and cheerful calls of garden birds, she need only close her eyes to feel the horror of waiting helpless for her death in the bottom of the boat.

"Would you agree, then, that you owe me your life?"

"As does Reynold. As does Clement VI." Juliana studied Raphael's face carefully. There was no trace of his usual carefree smile.

"Then indulge me," Raphael said. "Simply provide me with answers, and you may consider the debt settled."

She waited.

"The assassination attempt by Reynold," he said, eyes boring into her face. "It was a sham, a fake."

Juliana hid a grin of pleasure. Perhaps she could allow her heart the luxury of joy in his presence after all. If he had reasoned out this much...

She kept her voice neutral. "Why would you say such a thing? Because you now know that Reynold is my brother? Because the pope greeted him and myself so warmly when we delivered Alfred?"

"No. You and Reynold could easily be traitors, just as Alfred was. For all the pope knows, Reynold might lie waiting on the roof again."

"Then why would you so firmly believe that Reynold did not intend to kill Clement VI?"

"It was common knowledge that I fed the pigeons each dawn without fail," Raphael answered. "After all, I was often teased for the habit by kitchen servants, ladies-in-waiting, other court jesters, and all the others who served the papal royalty."

"Yes..."

"If the master storyteller knew of this, it would be known too that at any dawn, then, I would have no choice but to see the assassin on the roof opposite my balcony."

"Could it not also be coincidence?" Juliana felt herself slipping into the role of a teacher forcing the student into patterns of logic. "What if Reynold did *not* know of your pigeons, and it was his and your misfortune that you saw him?"

"No," Raphael said, "your brother deliberately fired the crossbow bolt *over* the pope, then set the crossbow down before fleeing. And…"

Raphael shifted to face her more squarely. The sun fell directly across his face. Juliana told herself it was just her imagination, but he did appear to have grown older, wiser.

"He also addressed me by name," Raphael continued. "Yet I am certain we had not met each other before. I asked myself, could this man know me by reputation? I had to answer no, for the dark-haired stranger was not part of the royal courts nor a servant. My reputation as jester is only in the royal courts. And it is not likely one outside the papal palace should know of me by name, let alone recognize me."

"Your reasoning is sound," Juliana allowed.

"Sound, but tardy," Raphael said with a frown. "I should have thought this through much earlier. It seems, however, that thinking logically is not a habit I am accustomed to."

He straightened, and his gaze transferred past her to a faraway hill. "After much more thought," he said. "I also decided that if the attempt was a sham, it was still arranged by someone who knew the pope's calendar enough to know he would walk through the courtyard below at that hour and that morning."

He shifted his eyes back to her. She saw new strength and determination there.

"Almost," she said. "The truth is Clement VI himself agreed to stroll through the courtyard."

"As I thought," he said softly, so softly that Juliana leaned forward to hear his words, "you stood at your window brushing your hair to watch the assassination attempt. *You* are the master storyteller." He paused, looking at her intently. "Why all of this?"

"For good reason." Juliana found herself proud of Raphael. She had been forced to play him as a helpless pawn in events beyond his understanding and, against great odds, he had unraveled much of the mystery.

"For months, Pope Clement VI had been receiving threats assuring him if he decided to move to Rome, he would be killed. These threats had been left in notes he would find in his bed, under his plate at meals, at private gardens, all places to let him know that he could indeed be killed at any time. He soon decided there was a traitor highly placed in his royal court. How else could the notes appear where they did?"

"Politics," Raphael said. "Much at stake if Clement VI abandoned Avignon."

"And much if he did not. Until last night, Clement VI believed the threats truly came from those who wanted him to stay in Avignon. As we discovered, however, a small group of highly-placed English bankers were behind it, intent on making it look as if Italy were trying to force him back to Rome. Even Alfred did not know who really had hired him."

"This does not explain Reynold on the roof. Nor your presence in Avignon."

"No." Juliana smiled. "I had my instructions. I was to force the traitor to show his hand. By letting him believe that others meant to kill Clement VI, I hoped the traitor would take measures to know his new enemy. Imagine my surprise when I found out so soon. Alfred threatened to kill me if I declared your innocence in front of the pope. Alfred wanted you for himself. He needed to ask you privately who was behind your attempt on the pope."

"Demigius," Raphael said. "Alfred sent him to the dungeon to have me killed."

"Not until you answered some of the questions," Juliana said. "Alfred instructed Demigius to get you on the cliff's edge and frighten you into telling who had paid you to kill Clement VI. I had anticipated something of that nature."

"You had spies watching the dungeon."

"Yes. You were never in danger. Demigius was followed into the dungeon and away from it."

"That is little consolation." Raphael stood and began to pace. "You played me as the fool. I went running to stop a man with a crossbow—an act that could cost my life—and it was simply part of your game."

"Had I known you as I do now," Juliana said, "I would have informed you of all of it. But you were a stranger to me. And the traitor could have been anyone in the royal courts."

Raphael continued to pace. "I sat in the dungeon, afraid for not only my life but for my family. Certainly once I was there, you could have told me it was merely a game."

"I wanted to," Juliana said. "My heart broke to think of your pain. Had you reached Tarascon, all would have been explained to you. Please understand that. All I needed was for it to appear that someone—you as it happened—tried to kill the pope. You were to be taken from Avignon that night, as you were, and in the safety of another town, you were to be held until the traitor had been captured."

Raphael managed a rueful smile. "Only I abandoned my rowboat."

"Your return threatened to ruin everything. Demigius as our prisoner had confessed who hired him. Demigius had told us of the meeting place and time where we could capture the men behind the threats. Had you stayed away two more days, my plan would have been complete. Nor would I have worried so much about the gold on your head."

"The English bankers desperately wanted me dead."

"Yes. I intended to meet you at midnight and ask you to wait one more day until returning to Avignon. But Alfred followed me to the bridge, so once again it appeared I betrayed you."

"Why did Alfred suspect you?"

Juliana bowed her head. "He was wiser than I. The hunted was hunting the hunter. Little did I know that he too had Demigius followed from the dungeon. Once he knew that I had been part of Demigius' capture, he knew I was on his trail."

Raphael laughed. "It pains you not to have been perfect?"

"Clement VI's life was at stake." She raised her head. "The possibility of war across Europe. My mistake nearly cost it all, including my life and my brother's. Alfred, of course, had turned our trap for him into a trap for us. We arrived with a battering ram and pounded our way into our own capture."

"It strains my head to think of all of this," Raphael said. "Why did you leave me in the stable?"

"Again, because I wanted you safely out of the way. I had rescued you from the river and needed to leave you to assist in capturing Alfred. Yet I did not want you roaming Avignon. I had bribed the stablemaster once to say you'd purchased a horse and provisions. It was easy to bribe him again. With you in the stable, I could return to the palace and continue my plans. I would have returned the next day to release you and explain all."

She stood and approached him. She took his hands in hers and smiled gently. "You escaped the stable. Because of that, we are both alive today."

He stepped back from her. "I have not yet finished my questions."

The hardened look on his face bothered her greatly. Could it be he did not share the feelings she had?

"The silver in my room," he said. "You again?"

"Yes. Once your escape was made known, it seemed wise to let all of Avignon believe you indeed had attempted to kill the pope. In so doing, I hoped you would be discouraged from returning."

"You asked me about the silver I carried, knowing full well I was not a traitor."

"If I did not ask, you would have thought it strange. After all, I wanted you to believe I knew nothing of any of these events."

Raphael mulled it over. "I understand it now."

Juliana walked toward him. Again, she took his hands in hers. He did not pull away but held her gaze steady.

"Raphael," she began, "you are among the best of jesters in the land. My own eyes witnessed your feats of skill. Climbing rope. Running narrow beams. Escaping the stable. I doubt any athlete in the kingdom could best you. Yet..."

She struggled for words. How could she sum quickly everything she believed, everything she'd been taught?

"Yet, it is not enough."

Raphael remained silent, watching, unprotesting.

"To be sure," she said, "I have learned much over the last week. I thought matters of the mind could reign supreme, replace matters of the heart and body."

She blushed. "My heart, however, in your presence has shown me otherwise. And it was your feats of daring which saved my life. I can no longer pretend the heart and body matter little."

Raphael still said nothing. *Was he shutting out her words?*

She rushed ahead. "Thus it is my heart which beseeches you to consider carefully what I say next."

He slowly nodded.

"Raphael, too often men like you—who excel in the physical world—forget there is another world. Much less visible. The world of mind and soul."

His silence unnerved her, but she swallowed several times and forced herself to continue. "Thinking itself is invisible. One cannot hold thoughts, touch thoughts, see thoughts, smell thoughts. Yet thoughts exist, do they not? The same with your soul. To deny your soul simply because you have no visible evidence of its existence…"

"Love," Raphael said.

"Love?"

"You cannot hold love, touch love, see love, smell love. Yet it exists. I understand what you're trying to explain. This experience and my struggle to make sense of all of this have shown me that there is more to life than what a jester does and sees. Now it seems I have a hunger to learn what I have been missing."

Juliana would have clapped her hands in glee, but that would have demanded she release Raphael's hands first, something she did not desire.

"My childhood," she said, "was a childhood spent in seeking knowledge of mind and soul. Because of it, I understand that it is man's lifelong purpose. To always seek God."

"Yes?" Raphael correctly saw the hesitation building within her.

Could she speak her words loudly enough to be heard above the thumping of her heart? Because if he answered no, the pain would be unbearable.

"I would wish you might do the same, to seek God and embark on that journey we all must answer and too often ignore," she said. "For if our hearts travel in the same direction, Raphael, they might travel together."

It seemed like everything around her magnified as she waited. Clear and loud, the song of the birds. Dark and sharp, the shadows of each blade of grass. Angel bright, the sun across his face.

"Yes," he repeated, this time not a question.

"Tomorrow I leave," she said. "With Reynold, for duty demands I return to the courts of Normandy. Much more than duty, however, is my one desire to be with you again."

"And mine." Simple, dignified.

"But we can only be together if we share the same faith."

"Then I will seek God," Raphael said.

Juliana kissed Raphael lightly. She stepped back and smiled. "Yes," she said. "I await you at the end."

Historical Note

There was indeed a time when the seat of the popes of the Roman Catholic Church was moved from Rome to Avignon, France. This was a period from A.D. 1309 to A.D. 1378, also called the "Babylonian Captivity" by some historians.

Clement VI was the fourth of the Avignon popes, elected in May 1342. He died on December 6, 1352.

Sigmund Brouwer is a bestselling author whose novels include *The Last Disciple*, *The Weeping Chamber*, and *Out of the Shadows*. Among his books for children are the extremely popular Mars Diaries and the Accidental Detectives series. He, his wife, Cindy Morgan, and their two daughters live in Alberta, Canada.

Join the Supernatural Adventures of the Guardian Angel!

The guardian angel is working overtime in the lives of kids facing excitement—and danger—at every turn...

The Angel and the Ring

Brin, an orphaned, teenage gypsy, must learn to trust a mysterious girl and, ultimately, God to uncover the secrets of the one possession his parents left him—a ring.

The Angel and the Sword

When Raphael, a court jester, is falsely accused of attempting to murder the pope, his wits and his faith are all he has to solve the mystery in time to save his life and the lives of others.